Indulging Into Reality

Indulging Into Reality

Nadaa Emambux

Copyright © 2015 by Nadaa Emambux.

ISBN: Softcover   978-1-4931-9319-6
           eBook   978-1-4931-9320-2

All rights reserved. No part of this book may be reproduced or transmitted in any form or by any means, electronic or mechanical, including photocopying, recording, or by any information storage and retrieval system, without permission in writing from the copyright owner.

This is a work of fiction. Names, characters, places and incidents either are the product of the author's imagination or are used fictitiously, and any resemblance to any actual persons, living or dead, events, or locales is entirely coincidental.

Any people depicted in stock imagery provided by Thinkstock are models, and such images are being used for illustrative purposes only.
Certain stock imagery © Thinkstock.

Print information available on the last page.

Rev. date: 04/29/2015

To order additional copies of this book, contact:
Xlibris
800-056-3182
www.Xlibrispublishing.co.uk
Orders@Xlibrispublishing.co.uk

Contents

Chapter 1: Affliction & Isolation 1
Chapter 2: Reminiscence & Regrets 4
Chapter 3: Release & Recreate 6
Chapter 4: Do's & Dears 9
Chapter 5: Tales & Teddies 12
Chapter 6: Mist & Miseries 14
Chapter 7: Milk & cookies 17
Chapter 8: Whispers & Worries 20
Chapter 9: Grey & Turquoise 22
Chapter 10: Secrets & Stillness 25
Chapter 11: Lush & Loss 29
Chapter 12: Food & Ogles 32
Chapter 13: See-Dore & Dulce 36
Chapter 14: Toque's & Trays 39
Chapter 15: Armani's & Aventadors 42
Chapter 16: Presents & Past 45
Chapter 17: Words & Worries 49
Chapter 18: Cerise & coffee 53
Chapter 19: Clear & Keep 57
Chapter 20: New People & New Paths 60

Chapter 21: Date's & Desires 63

Chapter 22: Don & Dea 66

Chapter 23: Alys & Ails 69

Chapter 24: Pasts & Promises 74

Chapter 26: Kith & Kin 79

Chapter 27: Devoir & Duty 83

Chapter 28: Darkness & Decisions 85

Chapter 29: Silence & Suspense 89

Chapter 30: Calm & Calamities 92

Chapter 31: Agreements & Assumptions 97

Chapter 32: Faith & Reliance 102

Chapter 33: Limitation & Creation 106

Epilogue 109

Dedication

Inspiration is drawn from those that surround you.

This book is dedicated to my Parents and brother,
and to family and friends.

Editors; Azhaar Zohaib &
         Shabreen Choolun

Pictures: Le Prince (Cover Page) &
         Mohammad Salman Toorawa (Dedication Page)

Chapter 1

AFFLICTION & ISOLATION

Chances are given to people who are worthy of proving themselves to have changed.

Have I changed? Am I a better man now?
I stood at the door I once called home.
As I knocked, I wondered whether I would be given that second chance. Will my family ever forgive me for walking out on them 11 years ago?

They say we all make mistakes because we are human after all. But they also say that however big the mistake, the prospect of redemption never fades away.

"Why did you come back?" she scowled, "Go back to wherever you were!"

It wasn't like I was expecting a warm welcoming hug, but I had that flicker of hope that somebody else would open the door. But it was my sister, Nora, the one person who was affected the most by my leaving...

"Well hello to you too!" I smiled, taking a step into the house.

"Stop!" She thrust the door to close it."

"Please Nora," I pleaded, placing my hands on the door. "I need to speak to dad"

Something changed in her eyes, the anger faded, and it became moist. "Dad? Whose 'dad' are you referring to?" She asked.

"Please Nora, I've lost everything and I have nowhere to go"

I could see the pain and loss in her eyes like it had grown into her throughout these sorrowful years.

"And you come to seek our help? Where have you been when this family needed you?" She raged before slamming the door on my face.

I shouldn't have left... I see it now, leaving that thing with my sister to take care of ruined everything.

I walked around the garden, what should I do now? I tried knocking again, hoping someone else would open. Maybe my mum, I'm sure she would be happy to see me. But nobody did. I was left alone

I sat on the front porch, thinking about how my life had been the last 11 years. I left Barcelona when I was 19, with enough money to move to China and build myself a decent life. But last year, the company I worked for lost everything and had to cut down on people they hired. My talent was not needed anymore, and I was fired. For the past year, the money I had was spent on day-to-day costs, until I ran out, and never found myself another job. Having nowhere to go, I am now on this porch. Deep inside, I knew I would have to return one day, but I thought I would have to bring something back, make my leaving worth it. But all I brought back now was more pain, and a reminder of what my family has been through because of me, and the problems they had to endure.

When you betray the people you love, it's not the things you have done that hurt them most. It's the fact that it would then be a turning point, where they lose someone close to them.

Hours passed, and I waited, I should be patient. The memories of what life was when I lived here flooded my thoughts. Memories of her...

A car entered the main gate, and drove up to where I was. I couldn't see who was inside. Maybe it was my mum, she probably just got home.

I strode slowly towards the car, expecting her to come out and find me; she must have already seen me sat here.

The door unlatched, but it wasn't the jolly shorthaired lady that I remember, it was a young girl, and behind her, another girl. They looked nearly alike, wearing the same style clothes, seems they liked fashion, a lot.

"O-m-g, did you go to H&M? I saw this blue tank top you'd love! We should-" I heard the taller one say. They did not sound like they were from around here. They had American accents, like my family. Maybe they were family friends here to visit… They stopped talking when they noticed me. They both looked at me, probably wondering upon the thought of who this weird man was sat on the porch.

"Yes? Can I help?" she asked, she looked familiar. Did I know her from somewhere? I've seen those blue-grey eyes somewhere, but where?

"I'm waiting to speak with Mr. Kleon, is he home?" I asked

"OH!" she shrieked, as if I said something very wrong- "He passed away 2 years ago, I'm sorry you won't find him here"

"WHAT?" I shouted, without thinking. I startled the two girls, and they ran to their door. Wait what?? Did she just say my dad was no more? How did I never know this? How would I know anyway, nobody had any way to contact me, I never gave them the chance! The words created a weight; I could feel it in my chest, heavy.

Chapter 2

REMINISCENCE & REGRETS

I watched the two girls ring the doorbell, and this time, I saw my mother open the door. She ran to me and hugged me. "Why didn't you ever call? I waited, your dad waited..." she said softly.

"Why didn't you open the door for me all this time?" I asked, kissing her forehead.

"Nora, she doesn't want to let you in. I've been standing at the window watching you." She touched my cheeks, then my hair, "You've grown so much!"

She wasn't the same anymore, she looked feeble. Where was my mother? The chubby woman with ample cheeks I could pinch. That woman seemed to have been lost behind those doleful eyes...

"I'm sorry about dad, that girl told me" I wasn't sure how to say it, I felt faint, my head spun as if I was about to collapse, not knowing what I should do to make up to my weak mother. All these years, loosing so much, it all explained the vacant expression.

"That's Reesa" she said, pointing at the girl that hadn't spoken a word since she got out of the car. "Akira friend. She's practically family, around us every day."

Okay, so my mom didn't want to talk about my father's death. Maybe she doesn't like talking about it.

"Akira?" I asked, deciding it would be better not to talk about my father.

"Oh! Her! I thought you'd recognize her..." she said softly, looking deep into my eyes.

"No, why would I?" I was bemused.

Her eyes widened; "oh!" She paused and made a thoughtful face, "well, she's Nora's daughter."

Ok now I was even more confused. "When did Nora get married? Get a baby? How old is she?"

I got no response from my mother. She looked at me, and then went towards the house.

"I'm 11 I've never seen you be-"

"Akira! Get to your room now!"

That was my sister's voice; of course, she didn't want her daughter to be having a conversation with me. Where did she come from though? Couldn't she stay wherever she was? I didn't want to be thrown out again.

The two girls went away; they seemed excited about their plans for tonight.

"Nora dear, can you make sure your brother's room is ready?" My mom said kindly,

"Yes mom" Her eyes were glowering, but she didn't say anything.

We walked to my room, and not a word was said. I was wondering who this girl I just met was.

I entered my room, so many years later; it was the same as the day I left.

"Why is it still the same?" I asked, but she just glared at me with the glisten in her eyes and walked away.

"Wait, when did you get a daughter? You weren't pregnant when I left!" If Akira was 11, Nora had to be pregnant when I left! How did I not know that?

"She turned 11 two months ago" she replied and stormed off.

2 months ago? That's...

Wait... Was she? The reason I left? No wonder she seemed familiar! She had the same hair colour. The same eyes...

Chapter 3

RELEASE & RECREATE

With time, everything changes. Whether it is a good change or bad one depends on how it was before the change.

I sat looking at my dull room, it was dusty and it seemed like it was shut since the day I left. The bedding looked the same, the curtains drawn, exactly how I left it that night. Few of my clothes were scattered around the room, from the mess I made when grabbing what I needed before leaving.

How could they have never cleaned this room? I sat on the bed, wondering what to do next and suddenly I saw a dress, it was hers. I could still see her, in that dress. I opened the cupboard and there were all her clothes, I should get rid of these.

Sometimes a mere object is enough to bring pain. The memories they contain make them far more valuable than their use.

It took me 11 years to get over the pain, and seeing these clothes wouldn't help. We lived together only for a few months, but her things were in this room like it was hers all her life.

These reminiscences, they have their own way reminding you of something you try so hard to forget.

After I get rid of her things, how would I stop the memories that were engraved in every wall of this room, every bit of it?

The table where she sat and did her work, the side of the bed she slept on, the sofa by the window where she would sit and read books.

"Are you done?" I was tired and wanted the lights off; it was a long day at work. I have to work hard if we were to have this baby.

"No dear, 2 more pages." she said, without looking up. Nowadays, she spent her time reading books about babies, and shopping for one, even though she didn't know whether it would be a boy or girl. I watched her; she looked so beautiful, even when she had this serious concentration face on. She had begun to gain weight. The baby bump was starting to show.

"When's your next doctor's appointment?" I was never good with remembering dates; it made her angry, always.

"Tomorrow" she frowned "you should write it down if you keep forgetting, stop being so careless!"

"I never have time to write things you tell me, I'm always busy admiring you! Stop being so cute" I had to be careful with my words, I wouldn't want to make her angry, or upset her. It's my baby she was carrying after all. My mistake. But I will have to start accepting this new life, living with her, having a kid to bring up.

Memories, they had stopped when I indulged myself into my work, but that wasn't reality. And now I have to live with them again. I want to go away, away from this place, this room. I don't want to remember her. But was escaping the right thing to do? I did that for so long now, and it brought me no happiness, not one joy. Maybe trying to embrace reality would bring me some sort of peace. Maybe finding myself a job here would help get my mind off things. But then what? What will I do with my life? How will I ever forget about her? I know I would never forget about her. How would I stop that pain that comes each time I think of her, and move on?

There was a knock on the door, "who is it?"

"Cara, I'm here to clean your room." She spoke so softly I may have even heard wrong.

"Come in"

"Sir? Would you like me to clean your room?" She asked, looking around like it was the first time she entered that room. It should have been the first time; the last person that would have come into this room was a cleaner!

"So it's your room? I've been working here for 4 years, and I was never shown this room. It always remained locked." She said. Her voice was so soft I had to strain my ear to understand her words. She had a different accent. "Where are you from?"

"Poland, Sir."

"Saying 'Sir' isn't necessary, I'm Danial."

"OH! You're different from the others! You're like how Mrs Kleon was before!" she gasped. Why did she say that? Or, why did she say it like she was astonished? "How are you related to her?" she asked.

I did not see that question coming. She's been here for 4 years and she didn't know of my existence? Maybe nobody ever spoke of me. It was my fault after all.

"I'm her son, now help me get rid of some things" I answered blankly; she could help me get rid of Ariel's clothes and things!.

Chapter 4

DO'S & DEARS

It is never easy to begin something from anew. It takes time, effort, and mostly dedication.

Finding a job, setting up a new life in another country, leaving a life of luxury to start everything anew; living away from my family, my friends, everyone I'd known all my life. It was hard, but *nothing* was harder than what I had just done! 4 hours in my room with Cara, going through every inch to pack all of her belongings. I did not want to throw them away. I was not ready for that. After all, they were her identity, those clothes and objects. Her belongings, all of them, made my wife who she was. But for now, I just wanted to get it all out of my head, clear this sorrow from my head..

"There, that's everything packed. What should I do with them now?"

Just when I thought the day couldn't get any worse... I knew I had to get rid of all her belongings and yet I couldn't muster the courage to do it. Where should it all go? Should I consider throwing it away, or should I keep it?

"I don't know..." I whispered, I'd been fighting back the tears for a very long time but that was it! I couldn't hold it back anymore; I had to let it win.

I had to cry. I never did, not the day I lost her, not anytime in the past 11 years. Maybe it was because I never really felt her absence in those alienated spaces I stayed, there were no memories of her attached in the new life I had built...

But now that I was back, in the same room we shared our lives, where memories were made, I just couldn't hold it together anymore.

"Stow it in the attic..." I whispered, hoping she wouldn't hear and just leave it all here. I wanted to get rid of everything that reminded me of her, and yet I didn't! I didn't know what to choose anymore. But Cara heard me, and soon enough she was taking away those things that were dear to me. She could probably see the pain in my eyes and hear the pain in my voice when I told her what to do, so she stayed quiet. I knew she was watching me; Tears quickly rolling down my cheeks.

Why is it so hard for a man to shed tears in front of other people, but so much more acceptable for a woman to do it? Why?

"Wait! Not that! Leave that here!" I shrieked, as I noticed that gown. Seeing that dress brought back so many memories, sweet and dear ones, and the most important one too! I just couldn't get rid of it since it was 'the dress'!

"I do" she smiled, her pretty voice echoing throughout the church. Her greyish blue eyes were gleaming. I could see the truth in her eyes and felt it as she chanted her vows to me.

"I've known you most my life, as a best friend, and as a boyfriend for the past few years.

This is why I stand here today, not because of the mistake that we have made, but because I am sure, very sure I will be capable of taking care of you as long as I live. I will be by your side, in every situation,

I will try to bring serenity when there is distress,

I will try to bring peace when there is disagreement,

I will try to bring contentment when there is sadness

I will try to bring satisfaction when there is discontent.

I promise to devote my time to you, and our kids- our family.
Because, all I need is to build more memories with you..."

My eyes became moist. Those were the best words I have ever heard. Not only because it was coming from the beautiful girl who had just become my wife, but also the delicacy in each word felt like a feather brushing past every part of me before entering my heart, where it will remain, forever.

I had goose bumps, my lips quivered; it was my turn to say my vows. They were nothing compared to hers, I wouldn't be able to say such graceful words. I had spent days preparing for this, but I forgot it all...

The sound of my sobs brought me back into reality, I found myself burying my face in my hands, and giving in to the tears that have been waiting to come out for so long. She promised to be there for us, for me, and for the baby. Where was she now? Where was the baby? And mostly, where was I? I felt lost. As lost as I felt that day she had left me... I had the urge of running from it all again but if those 11 years taught me one thing, it is that I cannot run away from myself!

Chapter 5

TALES & TEDDIES

I felt my chest tighten, my heart was crying, why had she left me? All these memories were gushing back; good and bad...

"It's a girl!" the doctor said, analysing the screen. "If you look over here, we see her head, her hands..." she continued, outlining the form of the baby with her fingers. Our baby! I could see her on the screen, the most beautiful thing I have ever seen!

I glanced at Ariel; she seemed captivated by the image on the screen. I clenched her hands and kissed her forehead. She looked at me, beaming "Will you love her? Our baby?"

"Of course Ari, it's ours after all, our angel" I murmured into her ears, then kissed her cheek.

"She isn't a mistake; she's the best thing that has happened to me, besides finding you." She smiled.

"In 4 months, I'll hold this baby in my hands; I love her so much already." I replied, taking the envelope from the doctor

That night, we went home with a picture of our unborn baby. She carried it like it was a trophy she had won, showing it to everyone. We were proud parents already. The very next day, she went baby shopping again with Nora, *buying everything for our angel. She spent her days decorating the nursery, making everything pink and filling it with teddies...*

The nursery! What happened to it? I want to see it. I still remember how it looked like. I would watch Ariel decorate the room for hours, and add things she had bought that day.

I gathered up my courage and walked to the door...

Walking down the corridor with echoes from the past, my head was spinning severely. So many thoughts ran through my mind. I wondered what was behind each door that I passed; I haven't been here in 11 years. I reached the door that was meant to be the nursery. What did not cross my mind was that this could be the baby's room now.

For a while I stood there debating whether this was a good idea or not, but suddenly I picked up on some voices inside. As I strained my ears to hear what was going on, I heard a girl's voice

"But why?" she asked

"Just listen to us, he won't be here for long." it was Nora's voice.

"So I would have to start calling you mom now?" she sounded bemused.

"Nora we should... have..." It was my mother's voice. I couldn't make out what she was saying. She spoke too softly.

"He doesn't have to know! He is just a guest here" it was Nora's voice again and she sounded annoyed.

As I walked back to my room, I thought about what I had just heard. Nora asked my daughter to call her 'mom' for the time being. Why was she trying to hide the fact that Akira was my daughter? She told me that it was my daughter before she left my room. Then why this? It was all so confusing, I couldn't endure it, I just couldn't take it in.

They want me gone, but I can't leave now, not when there is no place for me to go to. I wonder if they told Akira I was her father. Maybe this was why she was asking Akira to call her 'mom'. Still, this did not make sense. I wonder if Akira knew I was her father. Anyway, I didn't care. I hated the baby that took my wife from me.

Chapter 6

MIST & MISERIES

"She will be here any day now" Ariel whispered. It was something she would say every night before sleeping. We were thrilled, everything was set and we only awaited the arrival of our angel. We hadn't thought of names yet; we decided that should be done after she was born.

"Any day now..." I repeated, my voice trailing off. Ariel watched me sleep, kept her hand on my cheek and caressed it. She could not sleep as she was not feeling well. The baby was kicking, more than usual. I wanted to stay awake with her like I usually did, but that I was tired from a long day of work. That same night, Ariel started having pains, and we had to rush to the hospital.

I will never forget the way Ariel's screams echoed throughout the house, and later, in the hospital.

It was nearing dawn, and soon the sun would rise, bringing with it a new day, one where my life will change completely, I will have a family of my own to take care of. My angel was going to be in my arms.

"Stop this pain, get her out of me" Ariel screamed, digging her nails in my arm. I felt helpless, I wish I could do something to stop the pain, I wish I could take the pain upon myself...

I caressed her forehead and kissed it, I held her hands tight. I knew there was nothing more I could do.

The doctor was checking everything when he suddenly gasped "Something's wrong!"

"What's wrong?" I asked, adding on to the strain that was already there.

Without saying anything, the doctor asked me to wait outside, muttering something about an immediate surgery. I did not want to leave the room, I held Ariel, trying to calm her, but a nurse was by my side, and followed me out of the room. Once, outside, I was met by my parents, my sister, and my brother. Far away, I could see Ariel's parents who had just arrived. The nurse asked us to be patient and informed us that the doctor will be out to explain shortly.

"Please sign the necessary papers so we can get on with the surgery, I'm afraid the baby's life is in danger. We may loose one of them" The doctor said it so calm, and went back into the room. I filled in everything and signed all the papers without thinking. This can't be happening right now. I was asked to prepare myself to choose which one I would like to save if it became necessary.

I could not choose! It was my wife, and my baby! How could I choose? I said I would not choose. Hours passed, and the surgery was ongoing. A few times a nurse would come out and update us with what was happening, but all I knew was I had to prepare myself for the worst.

It was nearing afternoon, and my mom came with some food. It was the last thing I wanted, so I refused to eat. Just then, the nurse came out and said; "She has lost too much blood and the pain is too much, I am afraid we may not be able to save your wife, the baby is fine, she will be kept under stern observation for a few days. We are trying our best to save your wife."

With that, she walked back into the room. I was happy my baby was fine, but I could not bear the thought of losing Ariel. If she is gone, I will have nothing. For the next few hours we all waited and prayed for the best. Everybody had gone to see the baby who was moved to another room. I caught a glimpse of it, but that was it. I did not want to see or hold her. I wanted my Ariel.

Finally, the doctor himself came out; "My apologies, I am afraid these are the last moments for your wife, you all may go to her if you wish. She had lost too much blood and I don't think we will be able to inject enough blood in time." The doctor's words sounded like echoes, I was numb, and I heard nothing my ears had deafened from a tragic state of shock.

I could not gather enough courage to see Ariel for the last time. Not in this state. Everyone ran into the room, but I stayed outside, I did not want to see this. I am losing my wife, because of a baby. The love of my life is leaving me. I cannot watch her go. I had to leave this place. Immidiently.

I ran out of the hospital without thinking, all I wanted to do was to leave everything behind. I could not face this pain. I could not stay, and see a baby that was the cause of my wife's death.

A whole day had passed in the hospital. With the surgery, and everything else. It was nearing dusk. I drove home as swift as possible, ran to my room and packed my backpack. I didn't know what I was doing or why I was doing that. All I could think of was to leave.

Taking money, booking a ticket to the first flight leaving this country, and grabbing my essentials, took me an hour. My flight to Venezuela was at 9, so I had to be at the airport within the next 2 hours.

I hoped nobody had followed me, I don't want this life anymore, I don't want to see the thing that caused my wife's death every day, and I wanted to leave it all.

Nothing could change the mistake I had done that day. After Venezuela, I moved to many different countries, and finally settled in China. I used my bank account, and had enough money, but my family could get my address because of that. And not to mention the tabloids, they followed me everywhere. Therefore, after a few months, I started to introduce myself under a new name, and chose China to settle down, as nobody would identify me there. Sometimes I would see how my family was doing in the news. The new hotels that were being constructed, and the new projects my dad was taking on.

Chapter 7

MILK & COOKIES

It's the familiarity and the peacefulness of a place that makes you call it home.

Waking up in my old room, after all those years, it didn't feel normal. What was 'normal' for me? I guess strange places and hotel rooms had become my 'normal'. But waking up today felt nice, it felt like home.

Looking into my suitcase made me nostalgic, everything in it smelt of Cape Town, my last stop and hope of finding a job before coming back. For the past 11 years, working in marketing, I moved around a lot. Egypt, Paris, China...

The sweet scent of freshly baked cookies and pancakes reached my room. This was what I would wake up to every morning when I was a kid. Mom stopped making cookies, when I, Georgio and Nora grew up. Who was she baking for now? Maybe Akira, she's still 11. I followed the smell along the corridor, and down the spiral staircase. The old wooden floors that creaked, the pine furniture that smelt of fresh wood; I didn't want to be around all this again. Who am I kidding? Why am I lying to myself? I missed this place. I missed wandering around this prodigious house we all grew up in. I wanted to return back to it many times. But I chose not to come back because of that baby. She wasn't a baby anymore. Did I want to see her now? I had not seen her since I figured out she was actually my daughter. I still despise her. Curiosity won, I walked into the dining room to find Akira sat gobbling her pancakes. She did not take her eyes off her food. Everyone else looked at me, and I was asked to sit.

Breakfast was as awkward as I had expected. The dining room had more people than I remember. The dining table was bigger, and had even more food on it. I looked around, everyone watched me, many of which were unfamiliar faces. I wondered if I should introduce myself. Nora stood up, and came besides me.

"Everyone, this is Danial, my brother who has just came out of hiding." she said with a dry voice. I regretted coming for breakfast already. "And Danial, this is my husband Finn,-" She said, pointing at a thin, dark haired man sitting at the table. He was dressed in a tux that looked very expensive. "My twins, Fiona and Nial..." She continued, showing me two kids, who like Akira, was sat gobbling down their cereal and their cookies. They glanced at me, smiled, and continued eating. They had Nora's eyes, the man's straight hair. They looked tremendously gorgeous.

Nora continued her introduction, but I heard nothing. I was watching the kids; they reminded me of myself at that age. They looked around six, and sounded very polite when they were spoken to. I liked those kids already. I wondered whether Akira was like them when she was their age.

Akira, my eyes looked for her. She was the baby that changed my life; my hatred for her had grown all these years. But I would always wonder where she was and how she looked like. And now she was sitting in front of me, a beautiful girl, with a pretty smile. If I hated her, why was my heart warming up when I watched her? Akira is such a beautiful name, I wonder who chose it.

I sat at the breakfast table next to Georgio; he hadn't spoken a word to me since I returned. With only two years difference between us, we would always hang out together. I missed him the most. We grew up together and went to the same school. Shared every secret, and always had each other's back. Nothing and nobody could separate us.

We think that we are so close to somebody, and nothing can come in between. But the worst of tragedies can happen at a blink of an eye, and be the reason of separation.

I had no appetite, seeing familiar faces after all these years, all I could think of was how could I mend all the broken links between everyone? Bring everything back to normal.

"How are you?" I asked Georgio, he was angry; I could see it, as I knew his habits. He blinked more and he became uneasy. He was never like this around me, ever! I felt a weight on my heart, like a stone. My brother, the person who was closest to me all my life was now nervous around me.

"Goo-d tha-anks and y-you?" He said, with difficulty. He was stammering. This wasn't good, he would stammer when he held a grudge against someone, or even hated someone! The weight in my heart felt heavier. I could not bear it anymore. I wanted to speak to my brother like before. I wanted it to be normal.

My eyes filled with tears, I could not stop it. "I'm sor-ry" Oh no, now I was stammering. I looked at my plate and played with the baked beans, trying to hide my tears. He heard me stammer and I felt his eyes watching me. He also knew, when I stammer, I'm nervous. I had to do it. I had to look at him in the eye. I lifted my head only to find his eyes glaring at me, full of anger and sadness. It wasn't a look I was used to, from my brother.

I smiled, or tried to smile. It probably looked like a fake smile, but I got no reaction from him. I waited, he took a last bite, and walked away "exc-cuse m-me" he said loudly. Now everyone heard him stammer, and they all knew the reason. Me.

Chapter 8

WHISPERS & WORRIES

"Georgio, what's wrong?" What was I asking? I knew what's wrong! I just ran after him, and didn't even think what to say. This can't be too hard.

"Don't speak to me," He snapped, increasing his pace.

"How are you? What are you up to these days?"

We reached his room; he opened the door, turned around and looked at me

"Laila, remember her? Weddings next week" he hissed.

"Really? Tell me all about it!" I chuckled, trying to act as normal as I could. But it angered him even more, and the next thing I saw was a closed door.

Okay, this will take a lot more work than I thought. What should I start with? I had to start somewhere. Anywhere.

Mending broken ties should be tended with utmost care.

I walked back slow but steady to the breakfast table, thinking about what I should do.

"In two days, we haven't told her though" I heard Nora whispering to the others, she sounded worried. I was in the kitchen, which was besides the dining room. I walked to where everyone was, but stopped when I heard a deep voice "For how long will he be here?" It should have been Finn.

Why did everyone think I was staying for just a few days?

"Not sure" Nora replied.

"We have to tell her, but where will she go?" my mother added.

I stayed behind the doors, listening to their conversation. They spoke of someone coming back and me having to go. They were hiding something from me. That is when I knew they did not consider me part of the family anymore. I used to be one of them, sat at the breakfast table, discussing family secrets. I wasn't listening anymore, I felt left out, stranded. I had to fix this. And I had to fix it now.

"Would she be angry?" It was a girl's voice, sounded like Akira. This new voice in the conversation caught my attention again.

"He may hear us." Nora cautioned, "I will speak to her."

Who was she referring to? I continued listening to their conversation. They argued whether my staying here and being around Akira was a good thing or not. I could not listen anymore, "Nobody told me Georgio was getting married!" I blurted, trying to change the conversation.

Everyone looked at me, shocked. Nora, my mother and Finn turned pale. I guess they did not expect my return to be so sudden. This confirmed my doubts; they were hiding something, something big.

"What are you guys talking about?" I asked, pulling a chair and sitting down.

"Nothing, you don't have to worry." My mom answered.

"When are you leaving?" Nora added.

Everyone was looking at me, expecting a number, but all I did was smile and reply "Never".

What followed was not something I expected; my mother stood up "You can't just come into our lives and leave whenever you feel like it, and expect us all to be okay with it!" She shouted, and left the room, her eyes full of anger and I could just see the hatred in it.

Everyone was looking at me with the same glowering eyes. "I'm sorry, excuse me" was all I could say, before retreating to my room.

Chapter 9

GREY & TURQUOISE

Nobody ever grows to become the person you imagined him or her to be. They become better.

"Is Ri home?" A girl asked at the door,
"No, she went to Paris for a few days, hasn't she told you?" He smiled.
"Oh yes! She did! I completely forgot!" She chirped, "Anyway, I've brought her something, won't you let me in?"
I heard the voices come towards me, "I'll invite myself in for tea" She giggled;
"Like always" He muttered.
They entered the living room and found me watching them, with a book in my hand.
Finn looked at me in astonishment for a few seconds, and then followed the girl inside.
"I'm pretty sure she told me she was coming back today! - Oh hi there, I'm Jessie," She said, extending her hand.

The ones that are friendly are the ones that are best remembered.

She looked familiar; I must have seen her somewhere. Maybe she was a distant cousin. I left the living room, sensing she was here to see the others; I would rather make myself scarce.

Passing by Akira's room reminded me of Ariel again. Somewhere in my heart, a ray of hope built like the sunlight at dawn, it crept slowly. Hope for a better life, as it did not hurt as much as I thought it would when I saw Akira. On the other hand, darkness fell, on the opposite side. That darkness was fear. Fear of never being forgiven. I blamed myself for leaving all these years and never coming back to check on everyone as I should have. Fear nobody would ever accept me here again.

Uncertainty is like vines growing around your heart and staying there. The anxiety grows like the leaves on those vines, and it becomes firm and impossible to detach.

My love for Ariel, at that time may have not been strong enough, or may have been too strong. I was a child, and I thought that running away would be the only way to fix everything. That child did not wait, did not attend his wife's funeral. Did not even think about holding his baby, not even once. That stupid, stupid child. And now, my family had rejected me, and were keeping secrets from me.

I felt a cold tear run down my cheeks; I wanted to make up for it. I had to speak with Akira; maybe she would tell me the truth. I should tell her who I really was. Would she believe me? Would she accept me?

A sudden burst of shrills and shrieks caught my ear. It was followed by hushed whispers. I rushed back into the living room thinking something very bad happened. But it was worse than that; I saw someone I did not think I would see, ever. She was not facing me, but I recognized every inch of her.

The turquoise dress she wore defined her silhouette. Chocolate brown tufts of hair loosely tied with pearls. Faultless from the back, I could not help but wonder how she looked like.

The silence in the room felt like a void, it gnawed at me, I wish someone said something. But they all looked at me with frightened eyes.

Then she turned around to see what everyone was looking at; *it was me.*

Ariel, my very own Ariel. Her features were perfect. Dark long lashes that surrounded her arctic grey eyes. The eyes that spoke a thousand words, words her glossed lips would not part for.

She curved the edge of her lips, forming a smile. It was a thin smile, but it made my breathing stop. The air was stuck inside me somewhere. I gasped, trying to shake off this dream; but it wasn't one.

Chapter 10

SECRETS & STILLNESS

The still atmosphere felt like the moment of silence when a glass menagerie is suspended in the air, just before shattering into pieces.

I did not know what to think. My Ariel was alive, and standing right before me. She was smiling; she was not shocked to see me. My heartbeat hastened, and everything else became a mere blur. I could not take my eyes off her. I yearned for a glimpse of her for all these years, and now I have got it. But I wanted more; I wanted to throw my arms around her, to see whether she was real, whether she was here, still with me. But my feet took only one step, before she lifted her hands, to say stop. I saw her other arm linked with another man. The pain of realizing she was not alone all these years felt like an invisible hand reaching for my throat. My chest felt like it was being compressed. I watched her, then him. He ran his fingers through his full black hair, showing his high forehead and more of his olive skin. With a strong jaw and a straight nose, he could be a model. His smiling eyes were the same colour as her dress, they had something in them, something I had seen in my own eyes a long time ago; Honesty, affection.

The few seconds spent 'studying' them felt like hours. But looking away from her made me anxious, so I looked back at her. I felt a nudge, it was Jessie;

"I know! She is gorgeous! But stop staring, she is to be married!" She whispered, but I could not take my eyes off her. I didn't care that the man besides her looked like a Massimo Dutti model whose muscles could take up a fight at any moment.

I wanted her; I wanted nothing but to ask her to forgive me. But how will I get that forgiveness if she was to be with another man? I felt like running, going far away, again. But how could I run? All these years spent running brought me back to where I began; it was time to face the reality of my mistakes. A mistake I now regretted more than ever. Why hadn't I come back sooner? Why did I leave without being sure?

"Excuse me" I blurted, and tried to walk away calmly until I was out of everyone's sight. I reached the spiral staircase and sprinted to my room. I was a coward, I had run again. I rushed to my room and locked the doors behind me. All I could do now was lock myself in and burry my face in my pillow and cry. A thirty-year-old man that had just run, locked himself, and was now crying.

The pain was almost physical, I her image stayed in my head. She smiled at me like she had erased the past from her mind. The years we had spent together, in love. Everything we had been through. My leaving, hadn't it affected her a bit? She had moved on. I could hear Jessie's voice in my mind saying '*to be married*'. It repeated in my head, and I could not help but wonder, how long has she known him? How was her life before that?

To get all these answers I would have to gather up all the courage I have; which is next to nothing. I will have to fix things with everyone. I walked to the mirror and looked at myself. There is no way I looked better than this man. I was a mess, literally. I have to mend my mistakes and win my family's forgiveness. And claim back my right in this family.

First things first, I had to fix my looks. I jumped into the shower, let the cold water run through my hair, and thought about what I should say and do. I had it all planned out. There was no time to go to the barber, so I grabbed the scissors, cut, trimmed and shaved.

I got dressed, choosing my best shirt. Not too formal, not too casual, just perfect.

After two hours, I looked back into the mirror; *good enough* I thought. I walked down the stairs. I could hear everyone's voices coming from the dining room. It was time for dinner.

When I entered, nobody turned to look at me; everyone was busy in conversations. I found myself a seated beside Finn who was trying to get Nial to eat.

"I won't eat what Fiona made! I don't like her!" He pouted, crossing his arms.

"Nial dear, your sister and your grandma made such delicious food. Besides, Fiona is too small to make it by herself; she only helped out-" He explained;

"Only helped out?! I made everything!" Fiona exclaimed.

"You can't cook, you can't cook" Nial giggled. And their little fight went on and on.

This little fight brought a smile to my face. The innocence in these kids made my heart light, I forgot all my worries.

"If I try to persuade Nial, Fiona gets angry; if I try to take her side, then Nial gets angry! What should I do??" Finn complained. He was talking to me; I did not know what to answer as I did not expect anyone to speak to me.

"let me help;" I smiled, " Fiona! Can I have some of your delicious food?" I asked.

"Of course uncle D; let me dish out for you!" she chimed.

"Uncle D?" where did this name come from.

"Mom told us your name but we can't remember it, so Fiona and I decided we would call you 'uncle D' can we?" Nial chuckled. Both their voices were like angels, they were such cute kids how could I say no?

"Of course!" I smiled. I then realised everyone else was silent, watching me talk to the kids. I could feel her watching me; I tried to ignore it all as much as I could.

I spent the rest of my dinner speaking to Finn, the kids and Jessie. Nora and my mother spoke a bit too. But they spent most their time talking to Ariel. I listened to her voice; it had not changed at all.

I avoided looking at her. I didn't want to see her again until later. Lowell, the man sat next to Ariel was a man of few words. Occasionally he would laugh at jokes and answer any question he was asked, but aside from that, I did not hear his strong British accent much.

After diner, Nora and Finn took the kids to tuck them in; I was left with Jessie. She spoke of college, and boyfriends; I heard only half of what she said. I figured out that her full name was Jessica, and she was Ariel's little sister. No wonder I did not recognize her. She was around ten when I last saw her. I wondered where Akira had gone. She wasn't there at dinner, doesn't she have a curfew? She should be back home by now.

My mother, tired, also went to sleep. On her way upstairs she whispered in my ear;

"I think you should also leave for bed. Please stay away from Ariel, she is finally happy".

I hadn't yet looked at Ariel. She was talking to Jessie about prom dresses. I took my mom's advice and excused myself.

In my room I wished I could hear her voice. It's okay if she doesn't speak to me, knowing she was alive was enough. I knew I had no chances. I unbuttoned the first few buttons of my shirt, untucked it and lied on end of my bed gazing at the stained ceiling and thinking of things I should consider to gain everyone's forgiveness.

knock knock

I heard a faint knock on my door. I dozed off sometime between now and when I had lied down. It felt like I had slept for hours. I wonder who it was at this time. I did not bother buttoning or tucking in my shirt, which had now ruffled. I looked sleepy; I could hardly keep my eyes open. I opened the door, and there she was, taking every ounce of sleep I felt, away.

Chapter 11

LUSH & LOSS

A white satin dress that trailed, her locks of hair covering her bare shoulders, a faint touch of lip-gloss, so much perfection right before my eyes. I choked on my own breathing. My legs felt numb; why was she here?

"May I come in?" she murmured, trying not to make too much noise.

I gave no reply. Moving away from the door and into my room, I could feel her walk close behind me. I pulled a chair and sat. I felt my ears and neck scorching; this was stressful.

Unable to take my eyes off her, I watched her pull and chair and sit at the coffee table. She picked up my box of green tea; "since when?" she asked, showing me the box.

I could not get my mind to think of an answer, "China" I blurted.

"Why did you leave?" She mumbled.

I hesitated; "I thought you died"

"What about our angel?" she whispered

"She took you away from me" I realised how stupid that sounded. And I knew that this was the wrong thing to have said.

She stood up, her eyes suddenly full of fury; "NO, you ran. You coward. All these years all I wanted was to hear the truth from you. Everybody told me you were a weakling, but I persisted. Now I know. They were right all along." She raged.

Being next to her after all these years, it felt nothing had changed. She talked to me the same way; she looked at me the same way. Or maybe, it was just my illusion.

"I'm sorry," I could not think of anything else to say. I knew sorry wouldn't fix anything, but I had to say it at least...

She looked at me, a face red with anger, eyes full of rage. She pressed her lips and clenched her fist. She expected me to continue, maybe explain myself, but I didn't. What would I say anyway? She glared at me for a few seconds, lost her patience and stormed out.

What just happened? I just spoke to her, to Ariel; to the girl I thought was dead for 11 years, to my wife! My wife is alive, healthy, in front of me, and I could not hug her, show her how sorry I was, and show her how happy I was that I had not lost her that day.

But I did lose her, and together, I lost myself.

After the way she had spoken to me, I was sure everything was still the same. She spoke with ease, and her eyes had the same love for me, it had never faded. I wondered if I still had a chance. I hoped I did. But maybe she won't accept me again because I had abandoned our child.

Lying flat on my bed I buried my face in my pillow and thought. I thought about what I would do if I were in her place. Thought about her loss, and losing her, our baby. And now, losing her to this man she was 'to be married' to.

That next morning I woke up with a body ache. I had fallen asleep on my arms so I knew it would be numb all morning. It was too hot; all I wanted was to spend a long time in cold water, which would help me relax. I grabbed my things and went to the pool. It was still the same, the beautiful pool, covered by the shade of palm trees. Having a rich family had its perks; one of them being living in such a grand house with a pool.

I spent hours in the pool and lying in the hot sun with a book. Such a beautiful morning made me forget I was hungry.

"I want to swim!" I heard a kid shout.

"Yes me too daddy!" I could not make out which was Nial and which Fiona yet; their voices were very similar.

"I'm going to work darlings, when I'll be back I'll bring you both in the pool. Okay?" I heard Finn explain.

They walked towards me; "NO! Let's ask uncle D to bring us into the pool" Fiona exclaimed.

"Go on, you should ask him first" Finn said, and they ran to me.

Both with pleading eyes, and sad faces, "can you bring us in the pool?" Fiona requested. Nial put his tiny little hands on mine, "Please?" He murmured. How could I say no to such angels? I forgot about my grumbling tummy and stood up. I picked them up, one in each arm, and started walking towards the house. "Let's get your swimming gears"

They squealed with excitement and threw their arms around my neck. Walking by the pool, I jumped in, both of them in my arms. "We love you un-" Fiona started, but she could not finish as she found herself in the cold water. They looked startled for a few seconds and then burst out laughing. They giggled and talked about how much they loved me. I loved the two kids already. They took my mind off everything else. Who knew 5-year olds could do the job nothing and nobody could do? Make me forget everything else, and have a good time.

I watched them swim around and play with the water. I spoke to them about their toys and what they would do every day. We spent hours in the pool, until Nora came to call us for lunch.

Chapter 12

FOOD & OGLES

Clam, chorizo and white bean stew; one of my favourite foods. The soft clam flesh in my mouth, the crispy chorizo, it felt like heaven on my taste buds. Something I have missed over the years was homemade Spanish food. It made me forget about who sat around the dinner table.

I had spent the day wandering around the streets of Barcelona. The Gaudi architecture, the smell of fresh food from Santa Katerina market, watching the boats in Port Veil... And now, I was tired. I left the house trying to find a job, and came back with nothing. I don't want to enter the family business; I want to work on my own. I don't think they would consider giving me back my old job.

When you walk away from something at your own will, coming back without earning forgiveness is unreasonable.

"Dan, would you like some Bizcocho?" I felt Nora nudge me,

"Sure" I muffled my mouth full of the last bite of my chorizo.

I had gobbled up everything on my plate and took the dessert and ate it like it would be the last bit of food I would be having for a very long time. Appreciating each bite, feeling the suppleness of the cream cheese in my mouth. It was one of the best Bizcocho's I've had in years.

"Isn't it the best one ever?" Jessie chirped.

There is a point in everyone's life where everything feels right, days are blissful, and nights are delightful. Those are the days we most cherish.

"Ri makes the best food! We're so lucky she's a chef!"

My Ariel had become a Chef? I knew she loved cooking but it had been merely a hobby. Nora was watching me, seeing my confused face she added "Ari was in Australia for a few years for culinary school. And now, she is the head chef in 'See-Dore'."

Oh yes, *See-Dore*, our hotel. When I left it was the biggest hotel in Barcelona, by the docks with the view of the beautiful sea from each room window. I remember designing the furniture and setting up the place. It was one of my first projects in the family business. I would love to work as the product designer I once was, but nobody would accept me back in the business after everything.

I forced a smile and nodded, Nora could see how uneasy I was. I looked around the table and caught a glimpse of Ariel. Her hair tied in a bun, white eye shadow and dark lashes. Her defined lips brought out her cheekbones, and they looked flushed with all the praises she was receiving that night.

"Dan! Tomorrow, you should come to my meeting, I will show you what this family has been doing since you left" Nora said, interrupting my thoughts and ogles towards Ariel.

"Sure, I've got to find a job though" I replied, wondering why everyone was looking at me. And the most peculiar thing was; why was my sister being so nice to me? For the past few days she had been giving me emotionless stares, and today she suddenly wants to bring me around and show me what I have missed.

I caught a glimpse of Lowell who was watching me coldly. There was something not right with this guy. As much as he seemed perfect for Ariel, I had a feeling he was hiding something. Did he know the truth about who I was? I guess he does, given that a fully-grown evidence of our love is sitting right at this table. I decided I should make eye contact so greeted him with a nod, but got no reply. His face remained stern, and looked back at his food. He whispered something to Ariel, and her face froze. "Excuse me" She muttered and walked to the kitchen.

I watched her walk away, and looked back at Lowell, who seemed agitated. Maybe I should check on Ariel, I thought. So I finished my dessert as quick as I could, "I'm all done" I said, picking up my plates. Walking towards the kitchen, I hoped she was still there. Maybe she would want to talk to me. There was something that made her uncomfortable happening.

I found her standing by the window, looking out into the garden. I halted at the door; my feet didn't seem to want me approaching her. I tried talking, but the words were stuck somewhere in the back of my mouth.

Never take the fact that you are able to care for someone you love for granted. One day, you could be standing right before them, and you won't be the one wiping the pain from their eyes.

Tears on her cheek were glittering in the sun, and I could do nothing about it. I wish I could hug her, tell her I was here now, and everything will be all right. I will make everything all right. But I lost the right to console her 11 years ago.

"What's wrong?" I forced the words out of my mouth.

She turned abruptly, she hadn't heard me come in. "Why did you ever leave?" her voice was croaky; she wiped her tears and started walking to the door.

"I asked you, what's wrong?" I repeated, grabbing her hand. The touch of our hands sent shivers down my spine. My heart started racing, and I was sure she could hear it.

Here it was, the touch I've yearned for all these years.

She quickly pulled away from my grip and turned to face me. "He knows I came to see you last night. He didn't' know who you were before that. We had an argument because he thought Akira's father had died. So I told him the truth about you, about Akira, everything. I thought he would understand. But he became angry; I saw something in his eyes I had never seen before. He thinks you are back for me, so he threatened to call off the wedding and to tell Akira-" She stopped, her face turned pale.

She still trusted me; I could hear it in her words. I placed my hand on her cheek; "tell me everything, please" I took her hand, "I'm sor-"

I heard the door open, someone walked in. I let her hand go, and turned around. It was Nora; she was clearly not expecting to find us there, talking to each other.

Her eyes shifted between Ariel, and me. She saw the tears on Ariel's face, and quickly walked to her. She wiped her tears; "You don't have to speak to him now," She took her hands, "We can get him out of this house right away if he is bothering you." Looking at me, she continued; "Either you stay away from her, or you get out of here. You did it once, you can do it again."

I nodded, and took a step backward. Suddenly, I felt Ariel's hand on mine. I could recognize her touch until today. "Wait" she murmured. Turning to Nora, she continued; "Its nothing he said. Its Lowell, he said something yesterday and I need to speak to Danial about it."

Nora thought for a moment, and then replied, "No, I won't have you talking to him. Whatever is wrong, I am sure you are capable of fixing it with your fiancée. Bringing Dan into this will only complicate things."

I would have to choose a better time to talk to Ariel, not when anyone else was around.

Chapter 13

SEE-DORE & DULCE

I spent the whole morning walking around *See-Dore*. The place was even more beautiful than when I last saw it. The pool made of stone floors looked as natural as a lake; the water had reflection of palm trees. I remembered deciding the placement of the plants and trees around the whole hotel with the landscape designer.

When the surrounding is beautiful, your mood automatically replicates.

It was noon, and the sun was scorching. It felt too hot to walk around the hotel. I decided to take a look at the rooms. The furniture I had designed was still there; but it was all set in a different way. The rooms looked even more beautiful than when I had set it.

"These rooms, they are even more beautiful this way" I said, "who did this?"

Nora smiled; "Giorgio's fiancée; She's very talented, maybe you remember her, Laila, now they're working together"

"When will I meet her? She must be different now!" I wondered.

"It depends on Georgio. He stopped bringing her home since you appeared. I guess you will see her in the wedding next week" She said, in a matter-of-fact way.

"His wedding is next week? He mentioned that to me, I completely forgot. What is happening with the preparations then? The house is rather empty."

"Georgio and Laila are doing everything on their own. Most of the things are done. Ariel is taking care of the catering. Everything is happening in this hotel." Nora explained.

We stood in the hotel suite, the view was of the whole city, and it was breath taking. This room had memories, memories of her and me. We would usually come here on weekends.

"I'll go check on something; my next meeting will be soon. I'll see you later" Nora said, walking to the door. "By the way," she turned before going out of the room, "sorry about the other day. I thought Ariel would be upset that you came back, and nobody wanted you to know that she was still around."

"What changed your mind then?" I asked

"Well, I spoke to Ariel and she said she was okay with you being around. She had moved on anyway. I was happy with that. It meant I could have my brother back. You don't have to explain anything to me; I know and understand why you left. I wish you had stayed in contact though."

"I'm sorry, I really am. I'm glad she is happy now. Anyway, go on and have your meeting, we can speak later. I have a lot of questions." I replied.

"Sure. Later" She said, waving. She walked to the door and turned; "For what it's worth, when you left, I blamed Akira for a while. I lost my baby brother because of her. I would refuse to play with her, and hate the fact that her cries would wake the whole house when I was trying to sleep. But after a while, I picked her up, and I go the best feeling ever. Since that day, I started to love her as much as I love my kids now." She closed the door behind her with a slight smile.

They say when you grow up with someone, you think alike.

My older sister understood me, and she asked for no explanation. A little glint of hope crept into my heart. Maybe things would not turn out so bad after all. Maybe everyone would forgive me, and I will have my life back.

I stood in the Suite, studying everything. The wall colours and flooring were the same. They contained all these memories within them. But the room looked different, more spacious. Some of the memories were lost within these spaces.

"Morning Mi Amor" she whispered.

"Morning dulce" I managed to say, my voice was husky

"Your dulce needs something dulce, I'm hungry!" she complained

"Then go make yourself something, or order it from down" I yawned, planting a kiss on her forehead.

The second weekend since me and Ariel were married. Her baby bump was growing faster now. I placed my hand on it, "You're getting fat" I snickered and kissed her tummy.

"Fat? No! It's just..." She argued her face gloomy. "Its true, but its a good thing. My love is getting cuter," I asserted, kissing her lower lip.

I got out of bed and walked to the bathroom. I felt someone hug me from behind; "Breakfast can wait, for now" she breathed in my ear. Kissing it softly.

"Alright then, whatever mi esposa needs"

"Esposa sounds amazing! Finally you can call me wife now" she chuckled.

I lifted her into my arms and walked to the bathroom...

Soon, she will be Lowell's Esposa. That is, if he doesn't call off the wedding. Am I selfish to hope for her engagement to be broken? To want her back after I was the one who walked away?.

Chapter 14

TOQUE'S & TRAYS

I sat by the pool, gazing at the stars. These grounds were full of her sweet delicate memories. It was not so bad living in her memories. Now that I know she is alive and happy, I could live my life here, I needed nothing more. My heart became numb each time I thought of the past. It didn't hurt, nor did it make me happy.

Maybe I should stay here tonight. After being so close to the place all these memories were created, I didn't want to face the person. After all, as Nora had said, she had moved on.

I texted Nora not to wait for me, and closed my eyes. I listened to the serene sound of water in the pool splashing against the edges and spaying the plants. The water dripping from the leaves into the puddle it had created.

The sounds were calming. It reminded me of Ariel's sweet laughter, her happy smiles, and her soft whispers. How I missed her. I missed her for many years, and now, knowing she was around, I missed her more. I wished she was beside me at this moment, but she was probably with the other guy…I felt a pang of jealousy drowning my heart.

"Danial?" I heard a silvery voice call, and felt a soft tap on my shoulder.

"Yeah?" My voice was croaky. I opened my eyes to find a tall, beautiful lady in a white chef's uniform watching me. She carried her toque in her hand, and her hair was tied beautifully.

It was Ariel.

She looked concerned "You okay?" She asked.

"Please stop coming in my dream" I murmured, watching her. She gave no reply. I placed my hand on hers, but she pulled away.

This wasn't a dream, my eyes opened wide; she was still stood there, studying me.

"You slept here?" Her tender voice felt nice, I wished I could wake up to this every single day.

"Yeah-" I replied, and a sneeze stopped me from saying more.

"Gosh! Now you're getting sick! Come on, I'll get you to the room" She bossed, "you're always so careless"

I watched her hold my hand and pull me up. She held it and walked towards the rooms. I followed her, not saying a word. The only sounds I made were my constant sneezing. She walked me to the same Suite we would always stay in; it's only for family, so it was always empty.

She pulled the sheets and pushed me to get on the bed. Covering me with the sheets, she walked out of the room, "I'll be back with breakfast and some medication" She said, turning back to look at me. She looked around the room. She also remembered that room; I could see it in her eyes. Looking back at me, she muttered something that sounded a lot like 'Dulce'. She quickly looked away, and walked to the door.

"I'm sorry" I managed to breathe, between my sniffling and sneezing. She stopped, but didn't turn back. I knew she had heard me, but I did not expect an answer. She closed the door gently behind her. There was no way she would come back with breakfast now. Maybe she would send it with someone.

I got out of bed, grabbed the remote and a tissue box and got back into bed. I buried myself under the sheets, away from the cold and started to count how many times I would sneeze or use a tissue. Switching through the channels, I started to feel agitated. There was nothing to watch.

The volume was quite high so I hadn't heard someone walk in. I felt a hand grab the remote and type 5-2-4 and voila, my favourite. *Discovery Channel.* She remembered! Ariel was back with a breakfast tray, this time wearing her toque beautifully.

"You came back!" I whispered, mostly because I started to lose my voice, and I was shocked. "You look lovely in that toque"

"I knew that if someone else brings this, you won't have any." she replied flatly.

She uncovered the plate of food, and picked up the spoon. Adding some beans and a piece of omelette, she created the perfect mix and lifted the spoon to my mouth. "I can eat on my own u know?" I said in a matter-of-fact way. And opened my mouth.

She put the spoon back down, and started walking away. I quickly grabbed her hand; "but I prefer if you do..." I muttered.

She pulled her hand out if mine, "I've got work to get back to" She said tonelessly, and walked away.

Why did I have to say that? I just spoilt everything. She was showing that she still cared, and I sent her away!

I picked up the spoon and had my breakfast. I thought about her. There was something in her eyes. I could see the old flame for me was still there. She did not completely hate me. Maybe she will forgive me.

Chapter 15

ARMANI'S & AVENTADORS

I felt the soft breeze caress my cheeks and the scent salty water touched my lips. I had forgotten to shut the balcony door. The silky curtains flew around the room with the strong breeze.

I reached for my watch on the bedside table and checked the time. Noon, Thursday 23rd… I had spent three days in this room hoping Ariel would come with food and medication. But someone else always brought it. I felt better, it was no use sitting around in the hotel all day, I had to get back home.

Georgio's wedding is on Sunday, I have to find myself a tux and help with the preparations. It's the least I could do. I grabbed my things and headed home.

"Oh! We thought you ran away again!" Nora chuckled.

"I've been sick, on bed rest. Hadn't Ariel told you?"

Nora moved from the doorway and let me in, "Ariel? No! Did she know? The manager called and said you were there"

I looked around the entrance hall, all the doors were open, but there was no noise. It seemed empty "Where is everyone?"

Nora closed the door and walked towards the kitchen, "kids are at playschool; Finn, Lowell & Ari at work; Georgio's with Laila at the hotel preparing for tomorrow; and moms cooking…"

I made a confused face, "What's tomorrow?"

"Bachelors & hen's party. The guys will all be at the hotel club and girls here at home." She sneered, "oh, and you will see Laila tonight. We'll be decorating."

I spent the rest of the day finding an Armani tux; I hoped there was no dress code or I would have to go buy another one. Back in my room; I tried on my tux for the third time to check if it was perfect. It had to be. I had stopped dressing to impress, but now that Ariel is around, I have to start again.

It was a week since I had last shaved and trimmed, so I spent the next few hours perfecting my look. I hadn't gone for a proper haircut yet; I would have to do that soon.

The room was full of people; mostly in uniforms. One young lady caught my eye. Shining blond hair loosely covering her bare arms, tanned coffee-like skin, wearing a long blue satin dress with a belt around her waist. Older and more beautiful, I recognized her as Laila. "These tables should be covered with this silver silk taffeta, and on it these bouquets of orange flowers. And there…" She was a 15-year old school girl when I last saw her, and now, a young lady ready to be wed.

Silvery grey taffeta with orange flowers, I looked around at the partly decorated hall, it was beautiful. This girl had very good taste. I stood for a while watching everyone follow her orders, I could not find Ariel anywhere.

"Hey where you been all these days?" It was Akira, nudging my arms.

It was the first time she was speaking to me after I knew she was my own daughter. The baby I hated for all these years. But looking at her now, that hatred seemed to have faded away.

"Stayed at *See-Doré*, been sick." I managed a smile, "And how have you been keeping up?"

She made a sulky face, "Alright, can you bring me shopping? I've got to get Uncle Georgio and Laila their wedding gift. But nobody here is free to bring me"

I contemplated whether this would be a good idea; this the first time my own daughter was asking something from me, how could I say no? "Of course! I have to get a haircut and get them a gift too" I was not sure whether I would regret it or not.

"Cool! We can take the Crossfire!" She chuckled in amusement

Oh yes, I forgot about the cars in this family. Lamborghini's and Maserati's. It has been long since I drove one of those cars!

"Whose Crossfire is it?" I asked,

She looked at me with a confused face "Don't you know? It's uncle Georgio's second car. He never uses it. I'll go get the keys"

Before I could say anything, she ran off to find the keys. I wondered if Georgio would be happy lending me his car. He hadn't even talked to me properly since I had come back.

She came back a few minutes later, panting; "Uncle Georgio said we could take his car!" She caught her breath and started walking towards the door "He said you don't know where the new mall is, so I'll show u"

As the garage doors rolled up, I was exposed to a selection of super cars. I studied each of them, lined up besides each other at an angle. Grey Lambo, chrome green Maserati, Chrome blue Chrysler, Jet black Aventador, Red Evoque, and a white C-class Mercedes. These were all brand new, nothing like the cars I had when I lived here!

She watched me eye the cars in amazement, "Which car have you got?"

I looked at her, and looked down, ashamed "Nothing. I had an x6, but the company I worked for went bankrupt so now I have nothing."

She raised her eyebrows; "Then why did you ever leave? Gran was saying you used to help with the hotels"

Chapter 16

PRESENTS & PAST

The sound of the car reversing up was music to my ears. As I changed the gears and accelerated, I felt a rush of excitement. This was nothing like the 1976 Datsun I used to drive when I was here!

Once out of the gates, I watched the meter; 80...90...120...140... These were small streets; I probably should not go higher. I felt the car hugging the ground at each bend, not having to slow down.

The engine hummed with the blasting music; 180...200...240... I felt the adrenaline rush through me, and nothing was on my mind but speed. All my worries, memories, emptiness disappeared. I didn't feel lonely anymore.

'Andorra' the sign read. How did I reach here? This was around 150km from home! How much was I driving? I slowed down; look at Akira, whom I forgot was sat there. Her face was frozen, her hair was a mess and her eyes sparkled with excitement. She looked at me, and started to laugh.

I felt a soft wind brush my heart and weaken it. So this is what it felt to make your baby girl happy, how could I hate this angel for all those years? Those innocent eyes, that glistened, making me want to know more about her.

I turned the loud music off; "So, where is this mall you were saying?"

"We passed it long ago!" She sneered, "I want to learn driving. Gran once told me my dad used to love racing."

So they did talk about me…"What else have they told you about him?"

She made a gloomy face "Not much, just that he loved books and racing cars. Nobody talks about him and nobody answers any of my questions. Did you know him?"

I was not sure what I was feeling. My own daughter could not recognize her father when he was right before her; "Yeah, more than you think"

Her face brightened up "Will you tell me about him?"

"Of course" I managed a smile "Now, where is this mall?"

She looked around, "I don't even know where we are!" She chuckled in amusement "Let me check my GPS"

She picked up her phone and five minutes later, shrieked "*Pas de la Casa*! That's the best mall ever!"

I rolled my eyes "Well this is going to be fun…"

We spent the next two hours going into every shop, trying to find the perfect gift. "Our tastes are similar," She said, when we chose the same porcelain vase. Of course it's similar! We're related more than you think!

I listened to her chatter away about her school, her friends, her life being the "popular girl". Holidays she went on, her hobbies, her 'enemies', and what gifts she liked. I had to remember all this. I made a list in my head;

Katerina high school
Paris
Budapest
London
Karate
Swimming
Shopping
Hates Elina because she used her pen without asking, Debb was the math teacher's favourite and Jamie never asked her out

Clothes
Shoes
Contacts...
And the list went on...

My daughter was a typical cliché of a high school teenager.

Was that good?

We were back in the car "You haven't said a word" She said, raising her eyebrows.

I smiled "Did I get a chance to?"

She chuckled "Okay, tell me about you! Are you married? Kids? I never actually heard about you before you showed up!"

"Married, one kid" I said flatly

"Really? Why aren't they here with you?"

They are. You just don't know it. "Well, I hadn't seen them for so many years, we're not together anymore."

"Oh, I'm sorry" She said, making a sad face. "Let's not go back; I'm not invited to this party anyway."

I grinned, "Well, I have to get back! It's my brother's party. And don't you have a curfew? Won't your mom be angry?"

She crossed her arms and pouted "Ever since she decided to get married, something's changed. She's never around anymore. Always on holiday somewhere and too busy planning her wedding I guess." Looking up at me with big sad eyes, she continued, "I'm happy for her, I really am, but I wish she had more time for me. I wish it was my dad and not this new guy."

I was bemused "New guy?"

"Yeah, when I was seven, she decided to start dating. Since then, there's always been some new guy, some of them were nice, some of them weird. But she always seemed to find something wrong and break up. This one, she said he would be a good dad, so she was marrying him."

This was not the same Ariel I knew; "And how many guys has she been with? Don't you like Lowell?"

"Quite a few, I never counted. Never liked any of them. Probably because they were not like I imagined my father would be like." She smirked "As for Lowell, he rarely speaks to me, never asks about me. But mom's happy, so it's okay."

I asked no more questions. She didn't like Lowell, that's all I had to know. Changing the gear, accelerating, I looked at the meter again 190...200...210...240...

Ariel had been dating. She never found the 'perfect one'. Why wasn't I there with her? She would not have had to look for anyone! I would be right here with her. And now she found someone, and I was back. Will this change her life? Everybody says she is happy with this man. Maybe I should steer clear from her. This was my entire fault anyway; I have to let her be happy, I've caused her enough pain...

Chapter 17

WORDS & WORRIES

I sat at the bar with a glass in my hand. How much had I drunk for the last two hours?

Georgio hadn't said a word to me. I wished I could talk and have beers with my brother, celebrate his last night as a bachelor with him.

I recognized some of the guys from years ago, all his friends, and few of our cousins. They all seemed to be having a good time. After all, there were so many single girls around, models I guessed.

"Hola! Me ilamo Kat, cómo te illamas?" I studied her. She had straight brown hair, brown eyes, full lips and a sleek figure.

I smiled "Danial, nice to meet you"

She pulled a chair and sat beside me "I've never seen you before, who are you to the groom?"

I took another sip "His brother"

She raised her eyebrows "No way! He never mentioned you were coming!"

I turned to the bartender; "Refill please" looking back at her, I continued; "I just came back, been away all these years. He talks to everyone about everything?"

Why was she asking this? Wasn't she just one of the girls for this party?

She seemed offended "Everyone? You don't recognize me do you?"

I was confused "recognize?"

She smiled shyly "Katerina Martinez"

I laughed "No way! Kat? As in Dino's daughter? Last time I saw you, you were like twelve!"

Dino was a family friend. He was a good friend of my father since they had been kids.

She made a shy smile "Yeah, well, I grew!"

I looked at her again; she was definitely hotter than when I last saw her! Her cheeks were full, her body was curvy, and she had the smallest waist I had ever seen. Everything looked perfect...

Why was I looking at her in this way? I had not looked at anyone this way since Ariel! I still admire Ariel, but I'm not worthy of her. Heck, I'm not worthy of anyone!

I grabbed my drink and gulped it.

Everything started to become hazy.

"You are hotter than when I last saw you!" I told her

She grinned, "You too, come on let's get out of here"...

The hot blazing sun was too bright, why did I forget to close the blinds again? My head hurt, I wanted to sleep more. I got out of bed and closed the blinds. Walking back to the king size bed I noticed a mass of chocolate brown hair on the pillow next to mine. I was in too much pain to think, so I snuggled quickly back under my smooth coated duvet and fell asleep...

I felt something brush my cheek. Something smelt nice, pancakes, hot chocolate. My tummy grumbled, what time was it?

I opened my eyes to find the most beautiful angel sat beside my fluffy cloud like pillow with a tray on her lap.

"Wake up, you must be extremely hungry", she whispered.

I tried to remember the night before, but the headache that came with it stopped me. "How did I reach here?" I muttered.

"I brought you, last night. You were pretty drunk!" she chuckled

Did I sleep with her? What happened at night? "Thanks, there was too much on my mind I guess"

She made a curious face "Oh? Talk to me about it"

I could not think of Ariel and the others when I had a new problem here "Did we-?"

She cut me off "No, don't worry, you sure wanted to. But you were too drunk, I wouldn't want to" she sighed "not when you're drunk."

I heaved a sigh of relief "Thank you! And I'm so sorry if I said anything stupid!"

She smiled "Don't worry, c'mon and eat now"

I brushed my teeth, showered, then sat beside her to eat. There were two trays of food "You haven't eaten yet?"

She picked up her fork "No, waited for you. How are you feeling?"

I felt flattered "Not too bad, could be worse I guess. So, tell me about you. What do you do? Boyfriend? Married?"

She handed me a pill "Take this, the headache will go away"

She took a bite of her fresh chocolate waffle and continued; "Last night, you told me a lot, everything you've been through. I'm so sorry about everything."

I was baffled. I told her everything? So she knew how much of a stupid coward I was.

She sensed my hesitation "I'm going to be honest with you and share everything, I owe it to you now. I'm a marketing manager, Not married, No boyfriend. Well I had a few, but decided to take a break after getting pregnant and nearly killing myself"

I was dumbfounded. "Pregnant? Killing? I did not expect that!" was all I managed to say.

She looked at her plate and played with her food "Yeah, I didn't want the baby because its father was a total failure. I tried everything to get rid of it" She took a deep breath then continued, "I tried starving myself but it only made me weaker. I tried drugs, but it didn't kill it. My parents kicked me out, and I went to live with him. I could not get rid of the baby then, nobody would let me. For months I had started to live with the fact that I was going to be a mother, and I accepted it. Then one day, four months in, we had a fight. I took his drugs, and had an overdose. That did it, I murdered my own child. Everybody thought he had drugged me, so that got him arrested. I never told anyone the truth. I trust you, I guess. I can't look at myself now. I will never forgive myself. I tried so hard to get rid of it, but when I started loving it, I lost it"

Tears filled her eyes, "I was such a stupid kid".

I watched her. I felt her loss, "I'm sorry. I know what it feels to have made stupid mistakes. How old were you?"

She looked back at her plate "18."

I wanted to console her. She should not be blaming herself anymore. Mistakes happen. I placed my hand on hers, "Stop blaming yourself. You didn't want the baby, and nobody understood you. And later, it was his fault, not yours."

She looked at my hand, and wiped her tears "He was a drug addict, and he would hit me sometimes. I did not want a baby that would grow up and hurt people."

I moved closer to her and placed my hands on her shoulders. "Look, it's not your fault at all, it's his entire fault. And the baby, it's in heaven now, in better hands than it would be when entering this world. Your boyfriend would not have taken good care of it, being a drug addict"

She looked up at me, her eyes weary and full of regrets. They looked like mine. They were as lost as mine. Everything I had done suddenly came back rushing to me, and I remembered, today was Sunday!

"It's Sunday! The wedding!" I shrieked. "What time is it?"

Kat smiled; "Don't worry babe, you've still got a few hours until it starts. I got your things sent here, so you can get ready with me and we could leave together." She pointed at a bag at the far corner of the room then added "Oh, and I took the liberty of calling a stylist for you too."

Babe? That sounded nice! Should I work on this? "Thanks" I replied, with a peck on her rosy red cheek.

Chapter 18

CERISE & COFFEE

Cherish the moments spent in laughter.

"Check mate!" she squealed. For the third time, Kat had won. She was trying so hard; it would only be fair to let her win each time.

I leaned back and smiled, "You're good at this."

She snickered "I'm good at everything!"

I rolled my eyes "Oh really? How good are you at *café*?"

She winked, and walked to the kettle; "So, what are you thinking about work?"

Why is it that these questions follow me everywhere? I only brought her to the hotel to get my mind off everything that had happened yesterday. Being with all these acquaintances, asking more questions than they should made me regret being at the wedding. However, I remained calm, and was there for my brother. After the wedding, I could not go back home, where Ariel and Lowell were.

"Not sure" I frowned "I was supposed to go around and find something today, but here I am"

She took the kettle to the tap and filled it "I was thinking, maybe you could come work with me. I'm working on opening my own manufacturing firm, and maybe you could be the designer?"

"Serious? I thought you said you were a marketing manager? I would love to work with you, but don't you already have better people set for the job?"

She picked out two mugs from the cupboard; "Marketing manager for my dad's restaurants, but I've got a lot of free time and I really want to do this. Everything's more or less done; I'm on the recruitment stage now. And yes, I got two other product designers, but I'd let them go anytime! Come on! Not everybody has the chance to work with *Danial, Barcelona's best designer!* Have you seen the things you did when you were just 18?"

"Thank you! I owe you one!" I smiled "So, when do I start?"

"Tomorrow" she snickered "Help me out with everything, you don't have to start designing just yet"

"Thank you! The less time at home, the better!"

She poured the coffee and walked to the sofa I was sat on; "Sugar?"

"Two please."

I watched her as she bent over the coffee table to add the sugar, holding her hair behind her with one hand, and stirring with the other. She wore a purple mini dress; it showed off her curves just right.

"All these years and no boyfriend? How could the boys resist trying?" I muttered.

Soon after I had said it, I hoped she hadn't heard me.

She picked up the mugs and sat beside me. She handed me one, then shifted towards me. She sat so close I could smell her perfume, and it smelt good!

"Because I was waiting for you," She whispered, her brown eyes wide, locked into mine.

For a few seconds, I didn't move. I felt uncomfortable, with her so close. What was she trying to do? Was she flirting? Why wasn't I looking away? Her eyes were beautiful! Her full black lashes batted softly, giving me a glimpse of her violet eye shadow. My eyes wandered around her face. Her small nose, sleek and symmetrical. Her rosy red cheeks, Her lips... Full, cerise glossed lips...

She drew closer to me, I could feel her breath, and I could smell the coffee she had just sipped...

Before I knew it, I tasted her lipstick.

Suddenly, her lips left mine and she jumped from the sofa, with a shriek. Oh no! I had forgotten about the hot coffee mug in my hand! Some of it had spilt on her lap and burnt her.

"Sorry!" I managed to say, between all her screaming. I grabbed a napkin and tried to wipe the coffee off her legs. Her lean, tanned legs, ruined because of me!

When she managed to calm down, I called room service and asked for some cream for burn. They brought it a few minutes later, and I applied it over the reddened parts of her thighs.

"I'm so sorry," I muttered again

She placed her hands on my shoulder "Hey, its fine! Not your fault!" She was smiling. Okay good, she was not angry with me anymore!

She stood up, "I should get home" walking to the door.

"You angry?"

She smiled, "No Dan, I just need a change, I'll see you later!" She closed the door behind her.

I lied on the sofa. What was this? What had just happened? How could I be allowing this when my heart still belonged to Ariel?

Ariel, who had moved on, I did not deserve her. I did not deserve anyone! What about Kat? She was like me, she made big mistakes too, and did I deserve her?

At home, I found there was yet another party. Everyone was in the main hall, having champagne. Nobody seemed to have missed me. However, I was in no mood to join a party, so I walked up to my room.

Before I reached, someone called me from behind. I turned to find Lowell, in a tux. "Here are papers you have to sign," He said sternly, handing me an envelope.

I took it; "Thanks" I muttered. Before I could say anything more, he walked away.

Once in my room, I ripped open the envelope and there I found the papers I never thought I would have to see. I skimmed through the whole bunch of papers and a few words caught my eye; *Divorce, Custody, Heir, Land...*

Looking at each separately, I stopped at the one that read 'Dissolution of Marriage'. We were still married, I knew that, but what I has not realised is, until we had got a divorce, we would still be married, which means, her and Lowell could not get married. I grinned, this should be good, and I still could work on things.

I checked to see if she had signed. I hoped that she hadn't signed. If she hadn't signed yet, I could still have a chance.

She hadn't! The space next to 'Ariel Lavlinz' was blank.

Chapter 19

CLEAR & KEEP

What is not meant to happen, will never cross your path, leaving for you what is best.

It was raining outside. I grabbed my phone to call Kat. Today would be my first day working with her. But seeing the time on my phone, I realised it was too early to call her. I left the bed to get ready. After the nice hot bath, I heard a knock on the door.

It was Lowell, asking for the signed divorce papers. And behind him, was Georgio.

I tried to keep a serious face; "I won't sign," I said flatly. I wanted to grin and say 'HA! You can't get married without my permission'.

This was the first time we were having a conversation, and this was what he chose to talk about. And why was Georgio not speaking? I wanted my brother back, I wish he would speak to me, I could tell him about this.

Lowell frowned "Make it fast, stop playing games"

I clenched my glass, trying to keep calm. *Help me Georgio, please, be on my side.*

But Georgio watched us both with a blank expression. After a while, he spoke up; "Why won't you sign brother?"

He knew why, then why asks me? What should I answer? 'Because I love her'? If we were alone, I would. He just called me 'brother ', I felt my heart warm up to the fact that he may forgive me soon. I felt my lips twitch with a slight smile; "I won't do it until she asks me to"

"I see" Georgio grinned, and turned to Lowell; "Lowell, can I have a minute with my brother?"

Lowell nodded and walked away, and I followed Georgio to my father's study; the oldest room in the house. Furnished with pine antiques, the smell of Cuban cigars still lingered in the room, trapped in the wood.

Georgio pulled out a box from the drawer, opened it and offered me a cigar.

I smiled "No thanks"

I wasn't a big fan of cigars. He picked out one, and stuck it between his lips.

This should be important. He hadn't talked to me since I came, except for saying he is to be married. That too, was out of anger. Then why the sudden change?

He took a puff; "I don't like him, this Lowell guy"

"Why not?"

Taking a second puff, he continued; "In front of everyone, he acts all charming. But sometimes, he threatens people to get what he wants."

I knew there was something he was hiding. He could not be all perfect.

"Why is Ariel marrying him then?"

"Not sure, but compared to before, this is the best she's done. Anyway, that's not what we have to talk about." He paused, to take another whiff; "Dad left you as his heir, I took over after his heart attack because you were not here. But now that you are here, we have to sort out everything."

I watched him dumbfounded, heart attack?

"When?" I asked.

"When you left, he had too much stress because he was managing everything on his own. Nora and I started helping, but I was not as good as you. He would smoke more, which lead to his heart growing weaker. Two years after you left, he had his first mild heart attacks, then it became worse"

'Because you left', 'all alone'; these words kept echoing in my head. How could I do this to my family? I blame myself for my father's tragic death, for everything that has gone wrong. When I had left, I thought about nobody but myself. I thought my father a strong man, who could handle everything like he had always done. I never realised I was needed in this family, if I did, my father would still be with us today. Does everybody else blame me? I should work on fixing everything. I've been so oblivious. But no more…

Chapter 20

NEW PEOPLE & NEW PATHS

Letting go is the hardest part.

The whole morning was spent discussing the current and past situation of the business. A lot had changed, but the way everything was being handled was still the same. I have been watching my father do this since I was a kid; therefore, it would not be that hard to catch up on what I had missed.

It was nearly time for lunch. I had not had breakfast, so I started to feel hungry. Georgio's phone started ringing; "Yes?" he answered. After a very short conversation, he put the phone back on the table and turned to me "There's something I have to deal with at *Dorde-D'or*, I'll be back in a few hours."

Dorde-D'or, another one of the hotels. I would have to spend a few more hours just learning he names of the hotels and their locations, before getting into the details. I asked him which file contained all that information, and he pointed it out before leaving. I turned back to my files, dating from the year I had left.

A few minutes later, I heard a knock on the door, and Georgio walked back in.

"Anything wrong?" I asked.

"No, I've been trying to call you. Where's your phone?"

I felt my pockets and checked all around the desk; "Not sure, I guess it's in my room"

"Anyway, get it and come meet me down. I think you should come with me. You should probably start dealing with these problems too." He said, walking back out.

I went to my room, grabbed my phone and my coat. It was still raining heavily. Walking down the stairs, I looked at my phone *8 missed calls and 15 unread messages,* I read. I skimmed through it all, it was Kat, whom I was supposed to meet her at her workshop. I had forgotten to tell her I wouldn't be able to make it. I looked at the time, it was three already, and I was supposed to be at the workshop at nine. *'Sorry, something came up. Text you later.'* I typed, and pressed send. I hope she would understand.

I reached the car, a jet-black Aventador stood in front of me. What a beauty! It would be the first time I was in an Aventador. My dream car! Georgio wasn't sat on the driver's seat. He motioned me to get behind the wheel. He watched me gape at the car, and sneered "come on, I'm not sure what life you've been having all these years. But I'm sure you've at least *seen* one of these! You look like it's the first time!"

I walked to the driver seat "Never driven one of these"

I gripped the leather sport steering wheel, which was unusually soft. Studying the dashboard, the bright colours, white, red, yellow, and blue. There was only one dial in the middle, numbered between 0 and 370 all around, a white needle with a thin red line, pointing at zero. I had the sudden urge to make the needle reach 370. The fastest I had ever been was 270, and that was with Akira in the Crossfire. I put my foot on the aluminium pedals, it did not feel right. I removed my shoes, and then put my foot back on the pedals, I feeling the cold aluminium, and the carbon fire components. That felt better.

"Will we ever leave?" Georgio chuckled, interrupting my thoughts. He pointed at the control panel; where the start button was.

I lifted the red flap, and pressed the start button. I shuddered, hearing the engine whir for a split second, and then chortled. I quivered with the car, feeling the excitement rush into my feet.

Keeping my foot on the brakes. I pressed the accelerator and listened to the engine roar, watching the needle move around the circle briskly.

Leaving the breaks, I pressed the accelerator slowly, giving in to the humming sounds that filled my ears. Grasping the wheel, I rolled the car out of the gates, and onto the streets. The wheels gripped the streets as I increased my speed. *Empty roads, I need empty roads!* The excitement within me was increasing, and I could not be patient anymore. A few minutes later, I reached a very familiar road where there were barely ever cars, where I could test this lovely car! I pushed the accelerator fully, and within a split second, I clenched the wheel as hard as I could and felt my tummy sink.

Georgio showed me the way, and we finally reached the hotel. The grand iron gates swung open, and we entered the seven-star hotel that was decorated with palm trees. After, parking the car in front of the lobby, I walked in to find myself in a grand hall. The granite floors reflected the chandelier that hung from the high ceiling.

A short, bald man walked up to us and greeted us with a handshake. Georgio introduced me; it was the manager of the hotel. We followed him into the lift, to the 1st floor where the meeting room was. There, we spent hours discussing about the hotel's current situation. The hotel is based in a remote area by one of the beaches in south east of Barcelona. There was a neighbouring new development, and the noise complaints from within the hotel were increasing. This was affecting the amount of people that would come to the hotel. Something had to be done.

When we were finally done, it was close to dinner time. I glanced at my phone and there was a text from Kat *'Hope all's fine by your side, call soon x'*. I typed a reply, before getting back behind the wheels *'Heading back home now, dinner at Arola? It's a date'*. I had to apologise and decline the job she had offered me. But date? Since when was I setting up dates so abruptly? I liked her, no doubt, but it had been years since I went on a date. The only person I had ever taken on dates was Ariel. On one hand, I was trying to figure out what was wrong with Lowell, and not sign the divorce papers, and on the other, I was setting up dates. Was I doing the right thing by not signing the papers? Ariel had clearly moved on, maybe I should talk to her tonight, and if she wants that, I will sign.

Chapter 21

DATE'S & DESIRES

To make an effort is an act of kindness. Whether it be to others, or to oneself.

I stood at the mirror, and looked at the tall man standing before me. Brushed hair, clean and trimmed beard, crisp purple shirt, black pants, and polished shoes. Nothing too fancy, I thought. Maybe I should throw on a blazer; this was an elite restaurant after all.

My phone buzzed; it was Kat *'pick me up, no car'*. Glancing at the clock, I calculated the time it would take to pick her up, then drive to the restaurant. I would be late. Grabbing my wallet, I darted for the door, and ran down the stairs.

Ariel was walking up the stairs at the same time; "Where are you off too in such a hurry?"

"Got a date," I answered, with a blank expression, trying to mask the bitter feeling that was inside me. The feeling that wished it was Ariel I was taking on a date. Ariel, my wife, we were still married for goodness sake! But she had moved on, so why was it so hard for me to try and move on now?

She raised her eyebrows "Oh! Still dating are you? I thought after all these years, you should probably be married, and with kids" she said, in a sarcastic tone.

I clenched the handrails, I wasn't like her, and I had never gone on a date with anyone apart from her. I never even looked at any girl besides her. She was the one who could easily start dating other men, and now, found someone to marry. Walking down the stairs, I grabbed the car keys hung besides the door, and turned back to her. She had her back towards me as she walked up the stairs. "I am married, with a kid." I said flatly, and watched her stop abruptly. I wasn't sure whether she turned back to look at me, or ignored me, because a few seconds later, I was already by the garage, checking which car belonged to the keys I had grabbed. It was the Lamborghini, again. Not that I minded being in the car. It would be nice to test out the other cars, but I did not want to go back in for another key. What if Ariel was still around? The Aventador would do for now. Why was I even complaining? This was the best car in the world!

Revving up the engine, I rushed to the main gates, and out. Five minutes later, I was in front of Kat's house. I contemplated whether I should go in or just let her know I'm waiting outside. I tried calling her, but nobody answered. So I parked, walked to the door, and rang the doorbell. A tall, olive-skinned man opened and greeted me. He had curly hair and a cigar in his mouth. "Danial?" His deep voice sounded surprised.

"Yes Sir" I answered, shyly.

"I like what I see!" He said, "You look good! I would never recognize you if I bumped into you!" He said, offering his hand.

"Thanks, is Katerina around?" I asked politely, accepting his handshake.

He walked to one of the doors in the hallway and knocked; "Kat, he's here!"

A few seconds later, I heard her soft voice, "Alright, I'm ready" Her voice drew closer; "I'm so late!"

She appeared at the door. I gasped, seeing her in a hot pink midi dress, black silhouettes, and her hair straight. She had light makeup on, forcing all my attention to her curves that were clearly outlined by her tight dress. "How do I look?" She snickered.

"Gorgeous!" I gulped.

She giggled; "Come on, let's go" She grabbed my hand and led me towards the door "Bye dad! See you later!" She blew him a kiss, and closed the door behind us. Once outside, her expression changed and she stopped "oh my-" she gasped.

I smiled, and took her hands. She managed to stumble; "our ride?"

"Yeah, let's go, we're late!" I smirked, pulling it to the car.

She caught her breath; "I can't believe it! The famous Georgio Vasquez car!"

"Famous?"

"Yeah, in his interviews he always talks and shows off this car!" She muttered

"Okay! Anyway, get in now" I motioned her to the door.

At the restaurant, we were welcomed and given the best service. They recognized me from the times I used to bring Ariel there.

"So, when you gave me your address, I never realised I would find your parent's house." I said, whilst we both looked at the menus.

"Yeah, they took me back in after everything had fallen apart." She said in a matter-of-fact way.

"Steak?" I asked, pointing at the picture on the menu, and she nodded. After ordering our food, I turned back to her; "Don't you have your own place though? You're well off with the job and all."

She smiled and placed her hands on mine; "No, I would feel lonely if I had my own place. Plus, my parents want me around until I get married."

Once done with dessert, we walked back to the car and I dropped her home. I had enjoyed our "date". It was spent talking, laughing, joking, and getting to know her. She was a very nice girl, who worked very hard to make her dreams come true. She had a strong character, and since she had moved back into her house, she had become stronger and knew exactly what she wanted in life.

As I walked her to her door, I wondered whether we should kiss, or just hug and say goodbye. I decided I would go with a light kiss on the cheek, and leave. She stood at the door until I had driven away, wearing a bright smile as she waved.

Chapter 22

DON & DEA

The truth, once revealed, brings out pains that have been buried within.

Once back in my room, I tossed my blazer on the chair and threw myself on the bed. It felt nice to be back in my air-conditioned room. It was too hot outside, and after this long day, all I wanted was a good night sleep. Looking at the blank ceiling, thoughts rushed into my head. The date had gone well, she is a very nice girl; Pretty, clever, and she is well off. Then why can't I stop thinking about Ariel?

Ariel had moved on, but would I be able to move on? Should I even bother trying? Maybe I should. Signing the divorce papers would be a start. But then there was Akira, my daughter. Would she ever know I was her real dad? Do I want her to know? Maybe it would be better if she didn't know. I could try to spend time with her and get to know her better before saying anything. It would destroy her to find out that I had blamed her and hated her all these years. What if I lose her completely then?

The sunlight shone in my face, I had fallen asleep on the edge of the bed. My back was sore. I quickly closed the blinds, and went back under the covers. It felt so soft and warm. I remembered that I was supposed to speak to Ariel about the divorce, but I had no energy to do that just yet.

How much had I slept? I just closed my eyes! Why was someone knocking on my door so early? I opened the door, and there, right before me stood Ariel. Wearing a satin gown, looking irritated. "Had a nice night? Can I come in?" She asked bitterly.

Rubbing my eyes and yawning, I opened the door to let her in, "Please, come in! What time is it?"

"10, and why aren't you ready?" She demanded

"So what if I wake up at 10, 6 or 4? What's it to you?" I yawned.

"When will you become responsible? Georgio's been up since early, dealing with work. Lowell's been angry about something. He's been muttering your name often."

"And you're angry because?"

"Why is he saying your name? Have you talked to him recently?"

I smiled. I wonder if he had told her about the conversation we had yesterday morning. "How should I know? He is your fiancée, not mine!"

"Well, if he talks to you, tell me." She ordered, and walked to the door, muttering something to herself.

I watched her walk to the door and reach for the handle. As she did that, her sleeves moved and I noticed a purple patch on her arm. "Is that a bruise?" I asked.

She stopped, but did not turn around. "No, it's not" she replied. I could hear her voice quivering. I knew then, that there was something she was hiding. I wanted to know what. Why did I want to know? I should not be bothering about things like this. She had a boyfriend that should be taking care of her now. But I cared too, about her, and what happens to her. I always did. It won't go away in just one night.

I ran to her before she could walk out, and placed my hand on her shoulders; "Ari, tell me" I whispered.

I felt her stiffen. "I've got to go work," She answered, and started taking a step.

I reached for the door handle and closed the door before she could leave. Standing between her and the door, I asked again "Tell me, what's wrong?"

She looked at me blankly, but did not say anything. I would not give up this easily "Ariel, I know, you're hiding something!"

She closed her eyes, and pressed her lips. I was right, she was hiding something. When she opened her eyes, it was moist. "Lowell is not the same person I fell in love with," she murmured.

Love? She fell in love with this guy? How could she fall in love? Doesn't *love* happen only once in a person's life? Focus, this was not what I should be thinking about right now. "And?!" I asked.

She collapsed on the floor, "His real name is Dea Mariano." She sobbed.

Watching her on the floor, I could not help but going on my knees and holding her; "Mariano?" The name sounded familiar.

"Yes, son of *Don Mariano*" She continued sobbing.

I was dumbfounded, *Don Mariano*! Suddenly it came rushing back to me, who he was, and what he had done. He was the *Don* of Brazil. The mafia.

"Is he like his father?" was the only thing I could ask.

She looked at me, eyes full of tears; "Yes, I'm not sure how much, but he threatens, and he can use a gun. He asked me to come back to Rio with him, because he will be the next-" She put her arms around me and continued sobbing.

"Next what?" I tightened my grip around her. "Will he take over after his father?"

She nodded between her sniffles and sobs, and all I could do was press my eyes shut as the memories came rushing back.

Don Mariano was a very powerful man. He knew his way around getting what he wanted. He was very rich, and he killed people if he had to. Everyone knew about him, and nobody could ever stop him. Now, his son is in love with my wife. How will I ever be able to stop that?

Chapter 23

ALYS & AILS

People that we have once crossed paths with may not be the ones we would like to have part of our lives.

"*Don Mariano persona peligrosa,*" she wept. She was right, he was a dangerous man. A very dangerous man, and I should know, out of all people.

Placing my hands on her shoulders, I helped her to the sofa and sat on the floor besides her. She knew why I was quiet. She knew why this man was *peligroso*. She knew why I hated him. This man stole something from me a very long time ago. He had stolen someone who was very dear to me.

"*Nina*" I whispered.

Her eyes widened, she could see the pain in my eyes. The loss and the anger. I had to let myself cry, I was weak, and this man took my strength away. I placed my head on her lap, I let my tears go as remembered that day...

"Hello?" My father answered the phone. I stood at the kitchen counter trying to finish my cereal as fast as I could. It would be time to open presents soon, and I was expecting a toy gun. I watched my father speak on the phone and wondered who could be calling on Christmas morning? "Have you called the police?" I heard him say in panic. I stopped eating and stepped down from the chair. Suddenly I heard him shriek, and run for the door. I saw the phone lying on the floor whilst he grabbed his keys and headed for the door. It was cold outside, and he had forgotten his coat, so I ran after him with it. But I was too late; he had already reached the main gates and he was driving fast. I ran back inside and picked up the phone from the floor. On the other side, I could hear a lot of noise. Someone was screaming, and other people were talking loudly. "Hello?" I said, loud enough for the other person to hear.

"Danial? Lock the house dear, and don't let anyone in!" It was my mother, who was sobbing on the other end. She sounded scared. Before I could ask why, the line was cut.

I did what I was told. I locked the door and went to find Georgio. He was in our room, getting ready. I did not tell him what had happened, as he was only seven. I wished Nora was at home, she was older than us, she would know what to do. I told Georgio mamma and papa were not at home so we had to remain in the room and lock the door.

A few hours later, we heard a car coming in. I left the game we were playing and peeped through the window. It was aunt Jaida's car. But Aunt Jaida wasn't alone. My grandmother was with her.

"Hungry?" Aunt Jaida asked, with a blank expression. She usually greeted us with warm hugs, so this was new.

"Merry Christmas" My grandmother smiled, hugging us both.

"Nobody's home" Gerogio said, "Where is mama, Nora and Nina?"

"We know, they will be home soon, they went to buy more gifts for you," My grandmother explained, placing her hands on both our cheeks. I did not believe her. If she was buying more gifts, then why was she crying? And why did she say to lock the door?.

For hours, we saw nobody. Christmas was not usually like this. There was something very wrong. Granma told us we could open our gifts without everyone else, and go watch TV.

That night, we barely ate any dinner and fell asleep on the sofa, looking at the unopened gifts under the Christmas tree that were for everyone else. Granma told us mamma, papa, Nora and Nina were staying at a hotel that night as they are too tired to come home.

The next morning, I woke up, and I was on my bed. Someone had brought us in the room. There were noises downstairs. I yawned, and woke Georgio up.

"Is there a party? Is mamma back?" He asked in his sleepy voice.

"I don't know. Let's go see"

Standing on the stairs, we watched the entrance door as people walked in with flowers. They all wore black and looked sad. Each person walked in and said something to my parents, then walked into the main hall. Nobody had seen us standing there yet. Georgio grabbed my hand and pulled me down the steps. I followed him into the main hall, where people were sitting in rows and looking at something. There was a pianist, playing soft, slow music at the entrance of the hall. Looking towards where everyone was facing, I saw a big picture of my five-year-old sister hanging on the wall. It was decorated with flowers, and so was the floor all around it. "Why is Nina picture there?" Georgio asked.

I felt a hand on my shoulder, and turned to find my parents. They looked pale and their eyes were swollen. "I'm sorry," My Father muttered. "Your sister has left us"

I clenched my hands around Georgio's, who made a confused face; "Where did she go?" he asked.

"She has gone to God" My mother answered, and burst into tears. My father put his arms around her and whispered something in her ear. Before we could ask more questions, aunt Jaida pulled us to our room. She gave each of us a black suit and asked us to wear it if we wanted to come down. If not, we were allowed to stay in our room. But we had to say goodbye to our sister, so she helped us get dressed. We showered her with questions, but she replied nothing.

When we were ready, we went back into the hall and found Nora in a pretty dress sitting besides a big black box. She was crying and my mother's arms was around her.

"Can't I see her one last time?" I asked. "No, just say your goodbyes to her picture and she can hear you. She's in this" Uncle Sam replied, pointing at the box.

"I want to see her!" I yelled.

After a lot of yelling and crying, I was allowed a glimpse of her, but Georgio wasn't.

Uncle Sam opened the coffin, and there lied my baby sister. She wore her favourite white dress. But she was not the same. She did not look the same. There were bandages all over her. Her left arm was covered with a cloth, and her head had a big bandage wrapped around it, hiding her beautiful hair.

Her left leg looked bigger than her right leg. I wondered why, but I did not ask. Her pretty grey eyes were closed, and her fair skin looked pale. Her cheeks were always red and plump, but it wasn't anymore...

I was a nine-year-old kid who had seen and said goodbye to his baby sister whilst she lay in her coffin. I had many questions that were later answered. Georgio does not remember much of that day. But he does remember that he was not allowed to look at Nina. Later I explained to him what I had seen, and he had the same questions as me, what happened to her?

These questions were answered many years later. And the answers to all the questions were Don Mariano. He was *peligroso*, he was why my sister died. But he was not the only reason.

My father was doing business with him. He had lent my father a great amount of money, and asked for it to be returned before the end of the year. Two years had passed and my father had used that money to set up his business. The hotel industry was booming, and he could pay Mariano back. But he did otherwise. Not considering the threats Mariano had made, the business and all the money consumed him. He did not want to return anything. So on Christmas morning, when my mother and sisters had gone to find the puppy Nina was promised, their car was stopped on the road. Built men took my little sister and drove away. My mother had dropped Nora at her friend's house which was close to where they had been, and then join the Don, where the men had asked her to come.

My father got a phone call from her that morning, and she had mentioned that she was hurt and bruised. He went to find all the money he had lying around in the hotels, and took as much as from a cash machine. He did exactly as Don Mariano had asked, and brought twice the amount of money, to where they were. But when my father had reached, he increased the amount to five times and said he would hurt Nina. My father tried to find as much as he could, but there was still some money missing. Because of this, the men started hitting my sister in front of my parents. My father tried everything to get the rest of the money, but it was impossible. Banks were closed on Christmas day, so he could not arrange for a loan in time. Don Mariano grew impatient and left his men in charge of the situation, whilst he went back celebrate Christmas with this family.

These men, full of muscles, no heart, and no feelings were left to blackmail my father and torture Nina. They did not hit her softly, they were too strong, and so they broke a few of my baby sister's bones.

'They held her arm so tightly and slapped her, which was why her arm broke. They swung her around like a plastic doll, holding just her left leg' my mother explained, many years later. "That's why her hand was covered, it was completely bruised, broken, and there was blood all over." She continued, "When they were throwing her around, they accidently hit her head with a steel bar, and blood came gushing out," She wept.

The day my mother had told me the truth, I confronted my father, asking why he had done nothing all these years?

'Mariano is powerful, nothing could be done,' was his reply.

Something can be done, I thought, *something had to be done, and I will do it.*

But until today, I had done nothing. I could not do anything, my father was right. He took a piece of us, and walked away, and we heard nothing of him ever again. We received his condolences that day, and with it came a letter stating that his orders were not to kill the kid, so it was not his fault she had died. And with it, he had sent back the extra money that he had asked for.

"*Amante*, I'm sorry" Arielle whispered. She called me her lover, which had warmed my heart. Lifting my head, I looked at her "Hasn't he taken enough from me? Now he's taking you," I muttered, between my sobs.

Chapter 24

PASTS & PROMISES

The dreams and the wishes we carry in our hearts are the reason we remain smiling.

Ariel watched me with swollen eyes. She cupped my face in her hands and sighed;

"Help me" She muffled, between her sniffles and sobs.

"What can I do? Why has he come back into our lives?"

"Your dad had left it all on your name, and because you were not around, I could sign in your place. Lowell's plan is to take everything. He knew that, and marrying me would automatically give him power over everything. But now that you are back, he feared I would go back to you. His fears had become true when I told him I wanted another chance with you. That was he told me his real name and that I should be scared. He knows everything; he will take my angel from me. He will tell her we blamed her for us being apart"

"Our Angel" I whispered, "She's beautiful"

Since I had returned, this was the first time Ariel was showing that she still cared about me. But why did it have to be like this? Why was there another man in her life? I wouldn't mind if that man was a random person. Why was it Mariano's son? Wasn't life complicated enough? Hadn't we been apart enough? Now this man was around us, in this house.

If only we could have some time to ourselves and speak about Akira. Then I could tell her how sorry I am, and how much I had missed her.

"Why did he ask me to sign the divorce papers then?" I asked.

"He did? I know nothing about divorce papers!" She cried her eyes now full of astonishment. "Don't sign," she continued, "He is up to something, I don't know what it is yet, but please, don't sign anything he gives you."

"That's why I should not sign? No other reason?" I asked, looking into her eyes.

She watched me with intent "Mi primer amor" She smiled, "No puedo vivir sin ti".

That brought a smile; "I know I am your first love, but don't say you can't live without me when you have done it all these years!" I chuckled.

"And look what mess I had got myself into!" She answered, gently tapping my head.

She still loved me, I knew it. She had not said it yet, but she will soon. Once I get rid of Lowell or Dea Mariano.

"I'm sorry I left you, I was stupid," I mumbled, I felt my heart heavy. It was my fault all this was happening after all.

"Don't say sorry, we've known each other most of our lives, I knew you by heart then, and I knew why you left. I never blamed you for anything. I knew you would come back one day. I tried being with others to get rid of the pain and the loneliness. But then I fell in love with Lowell, and we had gotten engaged. I wish I had stayed single. Then, when you came back I would be all yours"

I watched her, feeling a weight lift from my heart. How could she do it? How could she blame herself for the mess that we are in now? How could she not be angry with me?

"You were angry the other day I spoke to you! You practically yelled at me"

Her face was serious again, and her eyes filled with worry "That's because he was there that night, he had brought me here and was listening to us behind the doors. I cursed myself for saying all this to you. But it was his words, not mine. All I wanted to do was throw myself in your arms and forget all these years."

I was surprised, I did not know it was his idea, how could I not see the fear in her eyes that day? Why hadn't I realised she was not being herself? But then again, how could I know she would not be angry with me? I had left her for so many years, how could I expect her to welcome me with warm hugs?

I kissed her forehead and she continued; "And in the hotel, he found out from the people there that I was in your room. Since then his people have been watching me carefully, so I could not come back to your room. That was when the threatening had started. Before that, he was commanding me and I would always listen, as it would scare me. When I asked him to leave, he didn't. I broke up with him, but he never went anywhere." She said.

Knocks on the door startled us both. My heart began racing, what if it was Dea Mariano? I stayed quiet, hoping the person would go away. But the knocks continued. "Who is it?" I asked dryly.

It was my mother; "It's time you wake up! Aren't you hungry?" She asked.

"Coming, one minute," I answered, trying to fake a sleepy voice.

"Open the door please. I need to speak to you." She said softly.

I looked at Ariel, and she ran to the bathroom. I opened the door and my mother walked in, looking around the room as if she was looking for something. "Where is she?" She asked, "I know she's here"

I smiled; I could not hide anything from my mother. "In the bathroom" I mumbled.

"I hope you two haven't been up to anything. She is to be married" Her tone was calm, as usual.

"No, I'm just happy she's talking to me now." I replied.

"I see," She answered, opening the bathroom door. "Ari, Lowell's on his way, he could not reach your phone so he called me. Get back to your room before he reaches" She explained.

"Oh! Please don't tell him I've been here!" She shrieked, and ran out of the room.

"You made her cry?" My mother turned to me with questioning eyes.

"No, just-" I could not continue, I did not know what to say.

"Lowell is a nice boy. He took care of her for a long time. Now that you're back, I really want you to be happy; you're my son after all. But you're too late. Please don't come between them. She will be happy with him. She needs this." She explained.

I wanted to tell her all about Lowell, who he was and why he was the last person in this world who was 'right' for Ariel. Would it be okay to tell her? It would bring back the pain of losing her baby girl; I did not want to see that. But she was my mother; I could not keep something so big from her, even if I wanted to. Maybe she would know what to do. The only thing I needed now was a hug from my mother and her soothing voice telling me 'everything is going to be alright'.

It doesn't matter how old you are or who you have become. The person that has taught you your first words will always be the person who could make everything better with an embrace.

My mother, the person who had always encouraged me, loved me, and forgiven me. I could not keep this from her.

"Lowell isn't who you think he is," I started.

"Oh really? And who is he?" She asked sarcastically. "Do enlighten me!"

"I'm serious" I put my hands on her shoulders. "Sit down please, and listen to me" She looked at me in confusion. She saw that I was serious, so she sat on the bed. I sat beside her and took her hand. "Lowell's real name is Dea" I paused and looked at her smiling face; "Dea Mariano" I continued. I watched her expression change, like I had expected it to.

"Maybe they have the same name, but they're not related" She managed to say.

We both knew whom she was talking about. I watched her blank expression and continued; "Dea Mariano is his son, his only son."

"No!" She gasped, "No No No No No-" She trembled, and her face was full of fear. "They took my baby, now they will take this one. No No-"

I pressed my eyes, forcing back the tears. I had to be strong. "Mom, we have to help her get out of this. He threatens her and have you seen her bruises? -"

She raised her hand, stopping me from continuing.

"I don't want to know anymore, I don't want to see his face, do whatever you can, send him away. Don't let him take my Ari" She cried. "I've lost enough already"

I held her hand, and wiped her tears "I won't, I promise".

Chapter 26

KITH & KIN

Growing up surrounded by siblings gives you the chance of having best friends that will forever be by your side.

I grabbed my phone to call Georgio, He answered with a few rings; "Why are you calling? I'm just downstairs"

"Haven't you left for work yet?" I asked

He laughed; "No I'm just packing. Leaving for our honeymoon today remember?"

I had completely forgotten about that. If I told him what was happening, he would leave everything and even cancel his honeymoon.

Not telling Georgio what had happened between me and Lowell/Dea Mariano, was probably the best decision. "Before you leave, just tell me what I would have to do and deal with"

Only a selfish person would take away the happiness of someone's honeymoon. Instead, I decided it would be better to talk to Finn and ask him what should be done next.

After that brief conversation, I went to find Nora to ask her if I could speak with Finn. I found her in the kitchen, and she told me Finn was with the kids in their room, and would be down for breakfast soon.

"How is it that you both live here?" I asked her,

"I never wanted to leave mom alone in this big house, so we both decided we would move in and help out. What business do you have with Finn anyway?"

I took some pancakes she had just made "Had to discuss something about the hotel. He handles all the accounts, he should know."

I heard Nial's voice "I don't want to go school today, please dad"

I saw them walk into the kitchen and Finn lifted them onto their seats.

"Good morning uncle D" Fiona coughed.

"Morning darling. Not feeling well today?" I asked, giving them both a kiss.

Nial frowned "If she doesn't go, I won't go. Pleaseee uncle D, tell dad".

Nora gave them both their cereal bowls; "if you stay home, you will get sick dear. Do you want to be sick and not be able to go into the pool?"

"Okay fine, I will go" He sulked.

Finn took a sip of his coffee "Come on Nial, I will drop you on my way to work"

"Are you going to *Dorde-d'or*?" I asked.

"Yeah, and Georgio told me you have some business there too, you could come with me" He offered.

Once we had dropped Nial at his school, I explained Finn everything that was going on.

"I can't do it; I want to punch him." I snapped.

Fin nodded, but said nothing.

I continued; "I wish i could do something..." My voice trailed.

"We have to be clever about this, he is just one person. We are a whole family, against that one person. So what if he is the son of a *Don*? So what if he probably is already the current *Don*? We have nothing to lose.» He said, with a reassuring voice.

My inner reason smiled, agreeing with what he had said, but I knew it was wrong. "We do have something to loose" I sighed.

He raised his eyebrows; "What's that?"

"Akira, he will take her away from me." I muttered.

"Dan, he has no power over her, she is still your daughter by law. Not his" He explained

"Yes, but what if he fills her head with crap? Will she ever accept me then? She would hate me. Forever." I croaked.

My inner reason was stomping around, trying to understand why I was not agreeing with Finn.

"Listen to me" He placed his hands on my shoulder, "Don't be worried, this is what's making him think he has power over you. Why don't you tell Akira the truth? I'm sure she will understand. Tell her, before Lowell reaches her."

"You mean Dea Mariano" I scoffed.

"Yes, whoever it is! Just go speak to Akira. Do it today, maybe this is the best time!"

"No, I have to speak to Ariel first, and see if she would be okay with this" I answered.

"I'm sure she would have no problem with her daughter knowing who her real dad is, if that is going to save her from the person she thinks is her dad right now." He said, entering the hotel gates.

He was right, Akira took Dea Mariano as her father, she knew no other father, so it was he that took her to the 'father-daughter' dance, and it was he who gave her everything she needed. It was he who held her in his arms when she wanted to cry.

"Here, take the car. She's been staying at her friend's house this week." He picked up a pen and wrote something; "Here's the address and her number. She has no school so go there before she leaves, just in case she has plans"

With that, I drove to the address and knocked on the door. A young girl answered, I recognised her as Reesa, I smiled "Hey, is Akira around? I need to speak to her"

She motioned me to enter the house; "You're Danial right? She's inside"

Once inside, a young woman offered me tea and biscuits. She was Reesa's mother. I declined politely, explaining that I had just had breakfast and was in a hurry."

"Hey Akira, can I speak to you for a minute?" I smiled. Her hair was tied and there were crystals holding each lock of hair. I saw her resemblance to Ariel. They had the same features, beautiful features.

"Are you going somewhere?" I asked.

"Yeah, we are getting ready for a birthday, is everything okay?"

"Yes, I just have to speak to you, but it's okay if you are busy. It can wait." I explained.

"Sorry Uncle Dan, I've got to help Reesa get ready, and we have to leave soon or we will be late. Can we talk later? Unless it's very important." She chirped.

I could not spoil her mood. She seemed exited and happy. Telling her something like this would make her worried and sad. This was not the right time. Hearing her say *Uncle Dan* hurt, for the first time, I wished she was saying *Dad* instead. "It's alright dear, go on, good luck! We can talk later" I smiled, and watched her run into another room with Reesa.

Chapter 27

DEVOIR & DUTY

A person's true character is only revealed with time.

He held the gun at her head with his left hand, and custody papers in the other hand "Sign now".

As I watched Akira lay on her bed fast asleep, my heart filled with regret. "How could you be that stone hearted?" I asked, my voice filled with pain and fear. 'Don't show him that you're scared!' my reasoning scolded. How could I not show fear? He asked me to give him my child, or he would kill her.

Should I accept what he was asking? He was not asking me to sign divorce papers, why wasn't he? Why custody papers? Maybe he would then be able to take Akira wherever he wants, and Ariel would follow her.

He frowned; "What's taking you so long? You're thinking whether you want to save her life or not?"

Obviously I wanted to save her life, but what then? What will he do with her?

Ariel was sobbing, "Sign it please" she pleaded. She had already signed, out of fear. Just showing her a gun did the job.

But why was I taking so long? Maybe it was because I had hated this girl for so many years. Maybe this was what was holding me back. But now I don't, I love her. I'm thinking of her future. What will happen if I sign this? Will he destroy her life or make it better? Maybe he will be a better father to her than I have been. Anyone is a better father than me! But do I want to risk this? Do I want another chance at being her father? Will she give me another chance? This should be her decision "Give me a day; let this be her decision," I whispered, pointing at Akira.

Dea Mariano watched me. His eyes widened, and became darker. A few seconds passed, he remained stiff, revealing no emotion. How could he remain so composed? He showed neither anger nor understanding.

Slowly, he relaxed his muscles "Okay, I will tell her the truth. And she will then have the decision. If she chooses to come with me, I believe you would want to be there too Ariel?"

I felt my heart lighten, but tried to remain focused and keep a straight face. I just bought myself some time to think about what to do next.

Lying on my bed I watched the ceiling, and tried to think about what I had to do 'tell her the truth' Fin's words. I will have to tell her now. Grabbing my phone, I dialled Finn's number. It was quite late, and everyone was tired, but this was urgent. Hopefully it won't disturb Nora.

"All okay?" I heard Finn's deep sleepy voice on the other end of the receiver.

"Yeah, just... Dea Mariano called us into Akira's room at 2a.m, and-"

He cut me off; "Meet me in the study, I can't talk here" He whispered his tone more alert.

Chapter 28

DARKNESS & DECISIONS

Being with a person that loves you is assurance that happiness will find its way.

I flicked the switch, and the room brightened. I squinted my eyes; this was too much light for this time of the night.

He was leaning on the desk, his expression impassive, and the gun still in his hand. Why was he here in the dark? I hope he leaves before Finn comes.

I heard footsteps at the door. Too late.

Dea Mariano watched me, but his expression gave away nothing. Glancing at Finn he started to talk; "Don't worry, I was just leaving" his voice was fierce. "If Akira does not choose me, you sign the divorce papers." He continued bluntly.

I nodded, trying to remain calm, and watched him walk out. Finn waited for him to disappear into the darkness, then closed the door behind him.

"He gives me the chills!" He muttered.

"I need a drink!" I muttered. "And sleep"
Finn walked towards the cabinet "I really think you should sign"
"He will take her away!" I gasped.
"Now tell me, what happened?" he asked.

"Well..." I ran through the main points of our conversation with Dea Mariano, and his threat. Finn watched me, making no comment. He was quiet for a few seconds, then turned back to the cabinet and picked out two glasses, and a bottle.

"It would probably be better than him coming up with another threat for you to sign the divorce papers" He poured something in two glasses.

"True, but why does he have to get everything he wants? Is there really nothing I can do?" I grabbed a chair and sat down.

He handed me a glass "First thing, talk to Akira before he does. Why hadn't you done that this morning when I told you?"

I took a sip, "I'll talk to her when she wakes up, and hopefully I get to her before Dea Mariano does!"

Finn nodded "Right, what if..." He paused for a moment and took another sip; his expression thoughtful. Then continued, "Maybe you should not tell her anything, tell Dea Mariano you will sign, and let him take her."

This was not what I expected; "You mean just let him take her away? Why would I do that? God knows what he will do to her there!"

He frowned; "Listen, Dea Mariano and his family have all been sent to boarding school. So he will have no power over her. Technically, she won't be around him until she is 18, then you guys can tell her everything, and she will make her own decision."

He had a point. "How about holidays?"

He had his thoughtful expression again, "Not sure, but until then, we can figure something out"

"I have to speak to Ariel" I muttered.

"She already signed! She expects Akira to go anyway! By the time you speak to her, Dea Mariano will have talked to your daughter already!" Finn snapped.

There was nothing else to discuss, so Finn went back to his room.

The bright morning light woke me. I had fallen asleep on the couch. I quickly checked the time, it was 06:30. There was a message from Kat, but I did not check it. I had to find Dea Mariano. Akira wouldn't be awake until 10; so I had some time.

Walking to Ariel's room, I wondered what time did he leave for his house? Did he stay? I hope he did not stay, and then maybe I could have this conversation with him over the phone.

I knocked on Ari's bedroom door, and waited. Nobody came to the door. She must still be asleep, maybe still tired from yesterday. I knocked again, slightly louder, and waited. Maybe I should not be disturbing her. I heard movement, and she unlocked the door and swung it open. She squint her eyes, she straightened her robe and ran her fingers through her tangled hair. A few seconds later, she must have realised it was me, and her eyes became more alert. "What's wrong?" she whispered.

"Everything! I can't believe you could sleep with all this happening!" I snapped.

Ariel bit her lip; "I'm leaving for New York today, and I want you to sign the divorce papers"

What? What was happening?

"What does he want?" I heard a sleepy rough voice from inside the room.

I studied Ariel's face, her eyes had fear, and she continued biting her lip. He must have told her something, she could not be willingly asking for divorce. "Tell *him* that he can take Akira, I'll sign, but not the divorce papers," I said blankly, loud enough for Dea Mariano to hear, and to join the conversation.

"Oh really?" he sounded amused, as he got out of bed and walked to us, putting his arm around Ariel.

This could not be right. Why was he acting so nice to her?

"Well then, I guess I'll take Akira and you to New York today!" He said, planting a kiss on Ariel's hair.

He was trying to show me that he was the one controlling everything, and she was his. Why wasn't Ariel doing anything? Why was she smiling sweetly at him? This could not be right!

She grinned "Family trip"

"Yes baby!" He answered, turning to her and putting both arms around her waist. She mirrored his longing looks, and put her arms around his neck. I could not watch anymore. This man had won, he was taking both of them away, and she looked happy.

Before turning away, I caught a glimpse at Ariel's hand, which signed thumbs up behind Dea Mariano's neck. I felt a little wave of relief, but a storm of jealousy scooped the wave as I watched Ariel plant a kiss on his lip.

She had a plan. I walked down the stairs to the kitchen. She seemed like she had everything under control. Did I mess it up? Was she going to leave alone with him and let Akira stay with me? Did I make it worse by agreeing to give Akira away too?

Chapter 29

SILENCE & SUSPENSE

We sometimes are forced to watch the people closest to us go, but the hope of seeing them again allows us to bear the moment.

"Will she be alright?" I asked Ariel, as we watched Dea Mariano hold Akira's hands and enter the airport. She waved one last time at Akira, "I hope so" Her voice trailed off and she broke into sobs. "This is the first time she is going far away without me"

"I wish I could do something to stop her from going!" I felt so helpless.

Dea Mariano was taking my little girl away from me. I spent 11 years of my life away from her, and now, the second chance that I had got was being taken away from me.

It would be hard, thinking about my daughter being raised by another man. Maybe he would do it better than me. But one thing I knew was that he did not love her! If he did, he would not have pointed a gun at her. If it were not for the business he had to attend to, he would still be here. We let him believe he had the upper hand by taking Akira away with him, which was better than anything else. Once in New York, we knew she would be safe as she would be living with a family friend who would take good care of her.

Like the rest of his family, Dea Mariano decided he would send Akira to a boarding school in England. She would be far away from him, which was good.

I asked Ariel about his sudden change in the way he talked to her. She flushed, and answered, "I know what he likes, so I convinced him I was in love with him. He said he would take me to New York today, so I had to think about something fast. I came up with this plan and talked him into boarding school in England. She will be safe there, I know it."

She was to leave with him and Akira, but she faked an emergency call from the hotel, and told Dea Mariano that she would have to remain at her job until they found a good replacement. "I told him I did a mistake by wanting to go back to you. I told him I realised my mistake when you would not sign the papers, which meant that you did not care about Akira. He believed me, and he loves me so he trusted me."

Dea Mariano knew that if he took Akira away, Ariel would follow, as she would want to be with her daughter. He said he would send her to a local school and she would live in his house, but Ariel had managed to convince him about boarding school, like everybody else in his family.

Back at home, everybody was quiet, and I knew what was in everyone's mind. They were all thinking about Akira.

"Finally I can be with you, no Dea Mariano around, but I am not happy yet. I am worried about Akira" Ariel muttered, before she walked up the stairs to her room.

It was quite late, and I was tired. I told everybody goodnight, and not to worry too much and went to my room. Akira was texting and calling Ariel, every minute as she had promised, so there was less to worry about. I wondered if that night I would sleep alone, or would I have Ariel by my side?

My question was answered when I opened my room door and found Ariel fast asleep, on one side of the bed. She looked so peaceful. Trying to make as little noise as possible, I quickly changed and snuck into the bed besides her. She was facing me, so I could watch her sleep as much as I wanted, and nobody could stop me this time.

I remembered how I would watch her sleep during my sleepless nights. She was so beautiful back then, and now, she was even more beautiful. I slowly moved closer to her, kissed her softly and lied back down. She made no noise, and did not wake up. She was probably very tired from the day.

Watching her, I drifted off to a peaceful sleep, where my whole family was together and the world was perfect.

I felt an arm around me, and I opened my eyes. It was already morning. Ariel was so close to me, her nose nuzzled the back of my neck. I took her hand and pulled it to my mouth, giving it a kiss, and placing it under my chin. How I missed her touch.

"You awake?" I heard her soft voice whisper near my ear.

"Hmm yeah" I replied, my voice breaking.

"I missed you" her voice full of lament.

I turned back around and looked at her beautiful eyes "me too" I whispered, drawing her closer to me.

"Don't leave me again," She whispered.

I smiled "Never" I tipped her chin up, and kissed her...

Chapter 30

CALM & CALAMITIES

The prospects of finding real happiness lies within the understanding and acceptance of those that surround you.

"What do you mean you've changed your mind?" I snarled.

A week had passed, and nobody heard from Dea Mariano. Ariel hadn't received any calls, but she would constantly send him messages to keep up her act and make him believe she was all his.

However, she would talk to Akira every minute as promised. Akira would tell her about her shopping, and visiting the country.

"I have to speak with you, it's important." He answered his voice calm.

"Well, I don't!" I snapped, and then cut the line.

A few seconds later, my phone started ringing again. It was from another number. I picked up; and there was a familiar voice on the other line.

"Hey, it's Kat, why aren't you taking my calls?" She asked.

"Sorry, been busy. There are a lot of things happening around here." I looked at my phone, and I saw Dea Mariano was calling again. "Listen, I will have to call you back" and I cut the line. I may have sounded rude.

Picking up the call; "Don't you understand?" I snapped.

"Hey, I don't want to be having a conversation with you, but this is important. I know Ariel's been lying. She had no intention to come with me anywhere." He explained.

I remained silent, I wasn't surprised, he was the son of a Don, he could see through Ariel's lies surely.

After a moment, he sighed, and continued; "I loved her, and I thought taking Akira would make Ariel come along. But seeing that it didn't happen, I decided to tell Akira the truth"

Now that, was something I did not expect to hear. I knew he would tell her one-day, but I did not expect it to be so soon. "And?" I muttered, trying to concentrate. I was stressed, how did Akira take it?

He was silent, then took a deep breath and said; "She ran away"

"WHAT? RAN AWAY?" I yelled, not being able to hold my thoughts anymore. "How could an 11 year old girl run away? Have you tried looking for her?"

His voice remained flat "Well, she's back with you, I thought you knew."

I could feel the blood rush through my through my body and into my head; "How do you expect an 11 year old girl to take a plane on her own?"

I heard him take a deep breath; "At the airport I told her who her real father was, and that you had left because she was born. I also told her that her mother had hated her for being the reason you left. Leaving out the part about how you thought Ariel was dead; I told her that you both had sent her away so that you could be happy. She ran off leaving all her things with me, which was why I thought she had gone back home. She never boarded the flight. I did not go after her, as I would come back for them both after a week."

My grip around the phone tightened with every sentence. He had lied to Akira, my daughter. She must have been through the worst pain after hearing all this.

When you find out a truth that has been hidden from you for so many years, it's the realisation that lies were told to cover up the truth that hurts more than the truth.

I did not know what to say, I sat on the edge of my sofa and buried my face in my hands. After a few minutes, I heard Dea Mariano again; "I will not bother you again." And he cut the line.

With trembling fingers, I dialled Ariel's number and told her everything.

"This isn't possible, she just told me she was going to bed! How could she be lying?" I heard her quivering voice mumble.

"Come home, I'll try call her and hopefully she will answer." I tried remaining as calm as possible.

I looked for Akira's number and tried dialling it, but nobody picked up.

The fear of not knowing is inferior to the fear of knowing.

I spent the next fifteen minutes dialling Akira's phone, and hoping she would pick up. But after a while, it would go to voicemail.

"Did you reach her?" I heard Ariel's panicked voice. She sat on the sofa besides me and sobbed. My mother heard us and came. She tried to console Ariel, and I told her what was happening.

"I told you he would take my girl away again! Why didn't you stop this?" My mother cried, holding my collar.

I felt like a disappointment, yet again. I had not been able to keep my family together. How could I have expected everything to fall into place? How could I expect to receive no punishment for causing so much distress to my family?

There was a knock at the door, I wondered who it could be;

Nora and Finn were at work, the kids were at school, and Georgio wouldn't be back from his honeymoon until tomorrow.

Opening the door, I found Kat who seemed troubled by something. "Hey Kat, is everything okay?"

I had not told Kat that I was with Ariel again. I had not spoken to her much since we had last met. After declining to work with her, I was busy with the hotels and never got around to calling or meeting her.

"It's important, can I come in?" She asked.

"Its not a good time, can it wait?" I answered softly.

I heard Ariel behind me; "Who is it?" she asked, putting her arms around me.

I saw something change in Kat's eyes as she watched Ariel's hand slip between my arms. "You two?" She choked.

I nodded with a smile, realising that I should have told her. "Is everything okay?" I asked again.

Her expression remained blank; "I'm sorry I disturbed, it can wait." She stammered, before turning abruptly and leaving.

Confused, I turned to Ariel and asked her what we should do next.

"I'll call all her friends and we will find her. She could not have gone far." Ariel breathed, walking back to the sofa.

"Call Reesa's mom first" My mother motioned.

"Hello?" I heard Ariel say; "I'm sorry to have disturbed you at work, but I need your help. I can't seem to get hold of Akira, and I was wondering if you knew where she was."

I took the phone from Ariel, and pressed the loudspeaker button so we could all hear.

"Yes, she is at the mall today, try calling Reesa's phone. Do you have her number?" We heard the kind voice of Mrs Sinso over the phone say.

"Thank you!" Ariel shrieked; "we will call her now" she said, before cutting the phone, and dialling Reesa's phone.

After a few tries, nobody would pick up; "Lets go to her house, they may be there." Ariel said, before taking her coat and the car keys.

Once at Reesa's house, we knocked, but nobody came at the door. We tried tracking Akira's phone, but it was off so it did not work. We dialled Mrs Sinso's number again and explained her the situation, and asked her to try and locate Reesa's phone. Frantically, she agreed and said she would leave her office and come home. A few minutes later, we received a text from Mrs Sinso saying that she had located the phone, and it was moving down Arinsol Road. She asked us to drive there as fast as we could as we were closer, and she would meet us there.

Once there, we were met by traffic. Remaining on the phone with Mrs Sinso, we managed to follow the location Reesa's phone was leading to. We decided it would be better to be in one car, so we joined Mrs Sinso in her car. After escaping the heavy traffic, we managed to catch up with the location the phone gave, and found that it was Kat's car. The windows were tinted, so we could not see what was inside. Suddenly, the car increased its pace and turned into a road. We tried following it, but Mrs Sinso could not keep up. Using the phone again, we turned into the roads that led to the phone. But a few minutes later, Reesa's phone had turned off, and we could not locate it anymore.

"Now what should we do?" Mrs Sinso asked.

I thought for a while about what Kat had to do with anything and why was Reesa with her? "She is going in the opposite direction of her house, where is she bringing her?" Ariel asked.

At that moment, my phone rang; it was Dea Mariano; "What now?" I snapped.

"I'm at your house and nobody's answering the door" He answered calmly. "My father is with me."

Oh no, did he mean Don Mariano? The person responsible for taking our Nina from us? I decided it would not be good to tell my mother about Don Mariano being at the door waiting for us.

"I think we should take two cars and drive around here to see if we can find her. Why don't me and Ariel take our car and you and Mrs Sinso go around together?" I told my mother.

"Okay dear" She answered.

Chapter 31

AGREEMENTS & ASSUMPTIONS

Compromises, and promises are what we have to deal with daily. It is never easy, but it is eventually worth it.

Once we were in our car, we headed home to meet Dea Mariano and his father.

We walked up to the front door, towards the two men standing with a cigar each. Ariel trembled, "They will force me to go with them" She whispered.

"No, I will not let that happen. They've taken enough." I answered, taking her hand.

Once we reached the door, I shook their hands and invited them into the house.

"What do you want now?" I snapped at Dea Mariano.

"I am here with my father, as he wanted to see who was the girl I was in love with." He stated calmly.

Ariel's grip around my hand tightened; "You want hotels don't you? Take it, take See Dore" She shuddered "Just leave us alone, please"

I watched them both; their expressions did not change. Don Mariano's face remained stern and thoughtful.

"You've taken enough from us already" I added.

Don Mariano moved his hands from the armrests and joined them both on his lap. "What is it my son has taken from you?"

How could he ask this? Doesn't he know what it was? Or did he do that to so many people causing our story to fade from his memory?

I took a deep breath and tried to remain as strong as I could; "Around twenty years ago, you took my sister from us. And now, because of your son, we can't find Akira"

Don Mariano leaned forward and his brows knitted; "twenty years? I cannot recall"

This angered me more; but I knew I should remain composed. "Nina, she was five. Your men-" I could not continue. The words were stuck in my throat.

Don Mariano's eyes widened, and I saw a flicker of shock pass through them; "Your father is Mr Kleon?"

"Was" I answered with a confused face.

"Oh, I am sorry" He answered shaking his head. Suddenly he stood up and continued; "You say my son is responsible for something?" He turned to Dea Mariano; "What have you done? I thought we were here to take your fiancée?"

Dea Mariano looked down and sighed; "Because of me, their daughter ran away. I thought by taking her, Ariel would come to me. But that did not happen." He explained.

Don Mariano pressed his eyes together; "Do you know who these people are? I was responsible for their loss many years ago. I have not gotten over it until today. Because of me, a five year old girl was killed." He exhaled, and then exclaimed "A child!"

Dea Mariano furrowed his brows and pressed his lips; "This is the family you had told me about? How do you expect I would know that? I saw my chance to having hotels here, so I took it. And now, I am not walking away without anything father."

Don Mariano turned to me; "I am very sorry for my son's behaviour. I will help you find your daughter, and he will cause you no trouble ever again." He rationalized.

This brought some hope into my heart. I turned to Ariel, who looked at me with the same smiling eyes. Finally we may get back our daughter and everything will be okay.

"No father!" Dea Mariano yelled, "I am not leaving without what I had come here for. If not Ariel, I want the hotels. I will not do as you say this time."

I watched them both quarrel, and I wanted nothing more than to ask them to leave and let us find Akira. A few minutes later, Don Mariano picked out his phone and walked to the corner of the room.

During that time; I turned to Dea Mariano; "I will give you one of the hotels. Please get my daughter back, and leave us all alone. This is what you had come for, and now, you can have it."

He looked at Ariel, and his eye lingered for a moment on her as he thought. "Okay" He finally replied, "I really do love you. But I guess I should not force you."

Ariel let my hand go and walked to him; "I did too" she smiled, "before I knew you had lied to me"

"I have called my men" Don Mariano was back, "They are looking for your girl and her friend right now. Do you know anything that could help?"

I gave him Kat's number plate, and where her parent's house was, which he then passed on to his 'men'.

We then moved to the office where I made the necessary calls and sign any papers required to transfer *Noches*, one of the hotels, to Dea Mariano's name. I also sent a brief email to Georgio explaining the situation in case he received any calls about the hotel. I thought that email would be the easiest way so as not to disrupt his honeymoon, but it had done the opposite. I received a call from him where he stammered questions before handing the phone to Laila, who spoke for him. She told us they were taking the next flight home, and that we should have informed her and Georgio what had been happening.

After that conversation, Don Mariano's phone rang, and I heard him give directions over the phone. After cutting the line, he turned to me "Your daughter and her friend are at Miss Katerina Martinez's workshop."

Why did I not think of that? Her workshop was where her car was going!

On reaching the workshop, we found my mother and Mrs Sinso waiting for us in the car. "She locked them in a room" Mrs Sinso cried. "Why is this happening to them? What did they ever do to this lady?"

Ariel comforted her, and told her everything was going to be okay, then turned to my mother who was looking at Don Mariano in fear and discomfort.

I placed my hands on her shoulders; "Don't worry Ama, he will help us get the girls, and they will both leave."

My mother nodded, and we all walked to the workshop entrance where I found a broken door. I heard screams from within the workshop. I recognized Akira's voice, and followed it. It led us to a door that was locked.

"Akira? Reesa?" I shouted, hammering the door.

Reesa answered; "We are-" and the rest was muffled.

I heard nothing from Akira, was she angry? I continued hammering the door until it broke.

Once inside, I saw Akira and Reesa in a corner of the room. Their hands were tied and mouths were covered. On the other side, Kat stood with a gun, pointed at me. "Don't come any closer, or I will shoot" She cried.

I put my hands up and walked slowly towards her; "I know you will not shoot me, please put the gun down and we can speak." I cautioned.

"Yes, You are right, I will not shoot you" She moved and pointed the gun towards the girls. "But I will shoot them"

"Please, no" Ariel and Mrs Sinso both yelled.

Behind Ariel were two men with guns, pointing at Kat; "Permission to shoot, sir?" One asked.

"No, No, Nobody has to get hurt here" I reasoned.

I saw a faint smile on Kat's face; "So you don't want me to get hurt? You do love me after all." She sang.

"No, I love my wife, why are you doing this?" I asked

"What?" She snarled; "I killed my own child once, and I will kill yours if you don't leave Ariel."

I heard gasps from behind me, and turned. Ariel and Mrs Sinso were both on the floor weeping. I ran to Ariel and placed my arms on her shoulders "Be strong" I whispered, "We will get out baby soon"

Suddenly I heard two loud bangs behind me, and after a second, a third gunshot.

Everything happened so fast; I turned around to find two men running to the girls who were crying in pain, and there was blood everywhere. On the other side, Kat laid on the floor, motionless.

I ran after the two men who had picked the girls up and were heading for the car. I could not make out where they had been shot because of all the rush.

Chapter 32

FAITH & RELIANCE

Uncertainty leads to stress. Receiving a long awaited reply lead to relief.

"Miss Reesa has lost too much blood, we are trying our best." The doctor informed, before heading back into the surgery room. Reesa had been shot in the stomach, and the doctor had come out of the room to inform us what was happening after an hour. Akira was in a different room, and the doctor was still tending to her wound. She was shot in the left knee.

Thirty minutes later a nurse from the room Akira was in appeared; "She will be okay, we have managed to remove the bullet from her knee. However, she may not be able to walk."

"Can we see her?" Ariel pleaded.

"Yes ma'am, you may, but she is still unconscious." She explained, before walking away.

As Ariel ran into the room, a nurse from Reesa's room appeared; "She will have to go through immediate surgery, please sign the necessary papers, and we will also have to do a blood transfusion as she has lost too much blood."

Hearing the nurse say these words reminded me of what had happened in the same hospital eleven years ago. Ariel was in that room for hours, and I had walked away from my family without looking back.

Mr and Mrs Sinso left us to do all the necessary arrangements, whilst I went to join Ariel in the room. As only two people were allowed inside, my mother stayed outside with Dea Mariano and his father.

"Wake up" I murmured, caressing her forehead. Her face was pale, and her make up was all over because of her crying.

Ariel picked up a wet towel and started to wipe her face. We spent the next two hours talking to her and waiting for her to wake up. It was nearly night, and we realised we had not eaten yet. But we did not leave her side.

"You know, this reminds me of the day you were here." I whispered to Ariel.

She came around the bed and put her arms around me; "Please forget about that day. We both lost a lot, and have been through so much since then. I can't even remember what real happiness was. What it was not to live in fear and pain."

My eyes filled with tears; "I love you" was all I could say, before kissing her on her forehead.

"Mom?" We heard Akira mumble.

"Baby, are you okay?" Ariel screamed.

"Yes mom, what is happening?" She asked, looking around the room.

"You were shot? Can you remember?" I asked.

"Why are you here?" She snapped.

Ariel caressed her forehead; "Everything Dea Mariano told you was a lie dear."

She looked confused; "who?"

"Lowell" I answered. "He lied, we don't hate you, we love you more than anything else in the world."

She looked at us both and started to cry; "I should have come home" She sobbed.

"No no no, don't cry, please" Ariel said, wiping her tears. "We love you, and everything will be fine now. Your father is back."

She looked at me, and back at Ariel; "So its true? He is-"

"Yes dear, this is your father. I will tell you everything once you get better" She smiled; "Now promise me you will not do anything stupid. You will get better and come home with us"

"Yes mom, I've missed you so much." She whispered.

"Come on, go back to sleep now, you need rest." I kissed her forehead.

"Reesa" She breathed; "Where is she?"

"She is perfectly fine" I lied, "You don't have to worry."

We called the doctor who said that she would have to remain under supervision for the next few days, until she is fully recovered.

Leaving her to rest, we went to find Reesa's parents. We were met my by mother outside; "She's okay, Mr Sinso is in there giving blood, and Mrs Sinso is by her side. She is still unconscious though."

I sat on the chair besides Dea Mariano. He and is father stood up; "We will leave now," Don Mariano said; "We will not cause anymore trouble, and I hope that your daughter's recovery will be quick."

We shook hands, and watched them walk away. Finally Don Mariano and Dea Mariano were gone from our lives. And hopefully, we will never have to meet them again.

As Mrs Sinso walked out of the room, we told her the visiting time of the hospital was nearing end, and we would have to leave. Both her and Ariel were to stay the night with their daughter's.

That night, I lay awake thinking about the day that we had had. For the past week everything was fine. Who knew things would escalate this fast, and there would be so many losses. As I wondered what had happened to Katerina, I drifted off to sleep.

The next morning, Georgio knocked on my door. He brought breakfast and asked me to get ready. as we would leave for the hospital soon.

That day, too, was spent in the hospital, by Akira and Reesa's sides who were both brought into the same room. Reesa had woken up in the night, and both girls requested to be transferred in a twin room if they were to stay in the hospital.

I watched them laugh and joke. The pain, fear and worries were wiped off their faces as they sang and talked. "I can't believe we are in this together too!" Akira snickered.

"I know right?" Reesa laughed; "Everything we do, we do together! Even getting shot and being in a hospital"

"We should take pictures of us right now and show everyone!" Akira chittered.

"Just imagine what everyone would say!" Reesa responded, before laughing, then placed her hands on her stomach "Oh my gosh please don't make me laugh so much, it actually hurts"

With that, Mrs Sinso was at her side asking whether she was okay. "I'm fine mom!" She giggled. "Why are you all so stressed?"

At that moment, I knew how strong both girls were. Even as they lay in the hospital besides each other, they found the time to joke and laugh instead of worry.

For the next few days, Ariel stayed in the hospital with the girls, and we all visited everyday. By the end of the week, the hospital room was decorated in flowers and cards that were brought by people who had come and visited them.

Chapter 33

LIMITATION & CREATION

What is bound to happen will eventually always find its way to you.

Two weeks later, both girls were back home. Reesa was able to walk as she was fully healed, and Akira was walking with crutches. That night the Sinso family joined us for dinner. As we all laughed and talked, I looked around knowing that finally, everyone was smiling.

That night, I knew Ariel was relaxed. Her stress and worries had vanished. With her daughter back home and in bed perfectly safe, she decided it was time she looked after herself. I watched her lie in the bathtub, and I could not erase the grin off my face. I still had not got over the fact that I was finally with the love of my life. After 11 years of being separated from her, and coming back to see her with another man, I could not have felt any worse. And now finally she was in front of me, and I could watch and admire her for as long as I wanted.

"Something funny?" She smiled, repositioning herself in the bathtub.

"You're mine, finally" I admitted. I hadn't had a romantic moment with her yet. I hadn't told her how much I loved her. How much I missed her.

She grinned "Finally"

We looked at each other for a while, before she broke the silence "So, will you just stand there or join me? This is so refreshing!"

My lips curved into a wider smile, and I walked to her, sitting on the edge of the tub. I traced my hand around her cheekbones, to her chin. Then slowly placed my fingers under her chin and tipped her head up. Looking into her eyes, I drew closer to her. "I love you so much *mi Esposa*" I whispered.

Her lips touched mine "I know" she smirked.

Standing, I unbuttoned my shirt, and she watched me "Changed a lot I see!" She giggled.

"Well, my girlfriend was my gym all these years!" I grinned.

With that, I dipped my foot in the warm water, and played with the foam, throwing it at her.

She splashed me with water, giggling. Her face glowed, and I my heart warmed by the sight of her happiness.

"I love you" She whispered, her lips touching mine, our eyes burning into one another.

Slowly, my lips found hers, and our tongue danced to the slow sounds the water made.

Epilogue

"Happy birthday darling" I sang to Akira.

"Thank you dad" She answered, kissing my cheek, and taking the gift from me.

"This isn't the only gift." I smiled; "I missed eleven birthdays, and you will get a gift for each of them."

"Seriously? Oh my gosh thank you! I love you!" She danced.

It had been two months since she could walk properly again. It was nice to see her without her crutches and bandaged knees.

"Where are our gifts?" I heard two squeaky voices demand; it was Fiona and Nial, standing with their hands on their hips and frowns on their faces.

"Today is Akira's birthday, I will give you both gifts tomorrow okay?" I laughed

"Okay!" They both chanted, and ran off.

"You will spoil these kids!" Nora said sternly.

"Do you want gifts too? Why don't I just take everyone shopping tomorrow?" I joked.

"Yes! Why not?" Laila chirped.

"Come on, I will be broke by the time I get you all what you want." I snickered. "I'll take the kids to the mall and let them buy their toys. We have to shop for little Laila or Little Georgio too, don't we?"

Laila was 5 months pregnant, and since she had moved in with us, the house was merrier. We had gained new family members, and more were coming soon.

However, we did lose some too. Kat's family had stopped speaking to us after I had visited them explaining what had happened. They apologised on behalf of their daughter, but asked us to remain as far from them as possible.

To find real happiness is an uneven road. The path may include losses and pain. But in the end, the peace that is unearthed is the reason we took this road in the first place.

Printed in the United States
By Bookmasters